REBELLIOUS PRINCE

CAPTURED BY A DRAGON-SHIFTER: A QURILIXEN
WORLD SHORT NOVEL

MICHELLE M. PILLOW

MICHELLE M. PILLOW® - MICHELLEPILLOW.COM

ABOUT REBELLIOUS PRINCE

CAPTURED BY A DRAGON-SHIFTER
BOOK 2

Welcome to the dangerous world of Qurilixen where dragon-shifters and cat-shifters rule as fiercely as they love.

Shifters are known to embrace their feral side, and it would take a very impressive female to tame his.

Cat-shifter Prince Rafe knows that technically he's supposed to be traveling to Earth to find a bride, but he doesn't see the need to rush things. While his dragon-shifter neighbors appear all too eager to claim their mates and settle down, he's all for putting that final moment off and enjoying his little trips through the portal. Yeah, yeah, eventually he'll have to marry and set a good example for his people because on his planet females are rare, and they need to have children and blah blah blah. But honestly, cat-shifters are known to embrace their feral side, and it would take a very impressive female to tame his.

Then he sees Jenna Kearney and all bets are off.

WELCOME TO QURILIXEN

Qurilixen World Novels

Dragon Lords Series
Barbarian Prince
Perfect Prince
Dark Prince
Warrior Prince
His Highness The Duke
The Stubborn Lord
The Reluctant Lord
The Impatient Lord
The Dragon's Queen

Lords of the Var® Series

The Savage King

The Playful Prince

The Bound Prince

The Rogue Prince

The Pirate Prince

Captured by a Dragon-Shifter Series

Determined Prince

Rebellious Prince

Stranded with the Cajun

Hunted by the Dragon

Mischievous Prince

Headstrong Prince

Space Lords Series

His Frost Maiden

His Fire Maiden

His Metal Maiden

His Earth Maiden

His Woodland Maiden

Dynasty Lords Series
Seduction of the Phoenix
Temptation of the Butterfly

To learn more about the Qurilixen World series of
books and to stay up to date on the latest book list
visit www.MichellePillow.com

AUTHOR UPDATES

To stay informed about when a new book in the
series installments is released, sign up for updates:

michellepillow.com/author-updates

NOTE FROM AUTHOR

If you're new to my books, the *Dragon Lords* are my bestselling futuristic romance series. The stories became reader favorites, and so I wrote things from their enemy's point of view in a spin-off series for the cat-shifting *Lords of the Var*®. Then they ventured off into the stars in the series installment *Space Lords*. Now, I'm traveling with them back to our contemporary time with the series *Captured by a Dragon-Shifter*, which you are now reading book two of. Don't worry, I have the series reading order on my website to help you figure it all out, MichellePillow.com.

To those of you not new to my books, readers have emailed asking Dragon Lords cultural questions since the first dragon-shifting prince released years ago. I have teased you with a lot of little hints of how the Draig found brides in "the old days". Many of you have expressed wanting to climb aboard the space ship and sail away into the future—which would probably take some cryogenic freezing and a lot of icy waiting. Well, before you start packing those sweaters... I don't want any of you going to that extreme, so I've brought your favorite dragon-shifters and cat-shifters to modern-day Earth. They don't live on our planet, but they have recently started to revisit.

For *Dragon Lords* and *Lords of the Var*® fans, *Captured by a Dragon-Shifter* is a modern-day prequel series to those first books. They take place long before the princes you know and love ever found their mates, long before *The Dragon's Queen*, in a time when the dragon-shifters and cat-shifters actually—wait for it—*liked* each other and hung out as friends. They also don't have Galaxy Brides to bring them women.

There's no one left to marry on their planet, and things are starting to get desperate. So please be careful when you go out at night, or else you might just find yourself *Captured by a Dragon-Shifter*.

Author recommends reading series installments in order of release for the simple fact she likes hiding little tidbits in the books as she goes, and it's more fun that way, though each book can be read as a stand-alone if you prefer.

To the Pillow Fighter Fan Club

Kansas City, Kansas

"Hello, *faes*, want to take a ride on my spaceship?" Rafe shot the Earth women a playful smile and wagged his brows. They giggled just as he knew they would. Even on his home planet of Qurilixen he had a way with the ladies—well, what very few single ladies were left on his planet, and the alien travelers who visited. What could he say? Charm was a gift. Half the time it didn't even matter what he said to them, as long as he dipped his voice and smiled.

"I don't care if he is crazy, look at him," one of the women whispered. She had no way of knowing his shifter hearing could pick up her hushed words.

Rafe was technically supposed to be looking for a

bride while on Earth being as humans were reproductively compatible. It was the whole reason the shifter princes were allowed to leave their home world. Rafe was part of the cat-shifting Var royal family who ruled half the planet—the fun half. The other half was ruled by the dragon-shifting Draig. As much as he liked his dragon neighbors, they were a little reserved and obsessed with planning the future. Since the portal to Earth was on their land, they were only willing to open it if the princes looked for life mates.

All the dragons ever talked about was mating and continuing the family lines...kind of like Rafe's older brother, Prince Ivar. For a cat, Ivar seemed to be missing the wild gene.

Rafe grinned. He was wild enough for both of them. His trips to Earth were solely for adventure. The culture captivated him. The plentiful sea of women fascinated him, especially since his planet lacked that particular resource—females. Men they had plenty of.

He didn't stop to talk to the flirtatious women as he went to the diner's counter. If he forgot to acquire cheeseburgers for the Draig princess, he'd never hear the end of it. Princess Eve was the first and only human to be brought through the portal and the only demand she ever made was for Earth food. She'd married dragon-shifter Prince Kyran. The union was a good one. It proved portal travel for brides worked and allowed the three remaining Qurilixian princes to continue their explorations offworld.

Rafe knew why their parents wanted them to mate so badly. Scholars estimated that the shifters would die out within a generation if women weren't brought to the planet. No matter how many babies a woman had, the vast majority came out male. Scientists tried, but no one could explain it. People were healthy, lived longer lives—much longer than they had on Earth—and for the most part thrived. They just couldn't conceive girl babies.

The downside of Kyran finding love after one attempt through the portal was that their royal parents were starting to get a little suspicious when no one else brought back a bride. Rafe liked Princess Eve well enough. She was what the Earth people called a spitfire. And, thanks to her help, he and his fellow shifters were able to blend successfully in to the modern human world. None of this meant Rafe was ready to find his own princess.

Since shifters had originated on Earth centuries

ago, they still spoke a dialect of one of the Earth languages, but so much had changed since they'd left, and many things had to be learned. What little the elders remembered about escaping to Qurilixen was outdated and filled with stories of shifter persecution and bloody war. For this reason, they hid their shifting abilities while traveling. Not counting a couple bar brawls when Rafe had tried to seduce a claimed woman—not that he could detect a mark or finger shackle on her to back up the man's claim— Rafe hadn't seen much by the way of Earth battle.

Night pushed its way past the broken streetlight to darken the diner windows. The waitress behind the counter came forward with her notepad to take his order. He leaned forward on his hands. "I'm wondering if you have a smile for me, sweetheart."

Startled, the woman blinked rapidly and then started to laugh. She swiped her pen at him before saying, "What can I get for you?"

"A dozen cheeseburgers and do you have something called cream pie?"

"Chocolate, banana, coconut—"

"A slice of each. To leave." Rafe turned as the bell on the door dinged to signify someone entered.

"I think you mean to go," the waitress said.

Rafe absently nodded as he studied the new

woman who entered. His accent made it easier to cover his English mistakes. He was about to answer when the woman pushed a hood off her head. Red hair spilled over her shoulders. The sides were clipped back to reveal small ears. A strong force hit him and he couldn't move.

"Evening Jenna," the waitress called.

"Hi Barb," the redhead answered. She turned, pretty green eyes looking past him to the waitress. "Usual please."

"Hey, spaceman," one of the women he'd flirted with earlier called. "Come sit with us."

"Joe's already started it for you, hon," Barb answered Jenna. "Be up in a minute."

"Thanks. I didn't have a chance to eat today." Jenna crossed the diner, pulling the strap of her messenger bag off her chest and over her head before shrugging out of her jacket.

"You mean you forgot to eat today. Again." Barb poured a coffee next to him and slid it toward the woman. "Sit down before you pass out."

Jenna came toward the counter. Rafe inhaled, detecting the scent of flowers in her hair. He stared at her. The sound of her voice mesmerized him. Jenna reached for the coffee and finally glanced up. He held his breath to hear what she would say to him.

Jenna arched a brow. "Your alien groupies are waiting for you, spaceman."

Rafe let loose his breath. "You know I am not from Earth?"

The woman stiffened, eyeing him as if he suddenly resembled the back end of a yorkin beast. She brushed past him and took a booth as far from the counter as she could get. Setting her bag on the table, she began rifling through papers and did not look at him again.

Rafe ignored the noisy women and they soon lost interest in his joining them. He sat at the counter to wait for his order and watched the redhead. She didn't look up, and he couldn't look away.

Jenna did not look like the Earth women he normally met. In clubs he could see at least sixty percent of a woman's body. Jenna appeared more reserved. Loose slacks and a blue striped button down shirt covered very lush curves. This woman hadn't reacted to his charming smile either. He found himself intrigued.

"Burgers be up soon. Here's the pie." Barb put a bag on the counter in front of him. "You're barking up the wrong tree there, lover boy."

"I do not bark," Rafe said.

"Whatever you say." Barb left.

Rafe lifted the bag of pie slices and made his move toward the table. At his presence, she mumbled, "Thanks. Just leave it on the table."

"You wish to eat my cream?" Rafe asked.

The woman gave a little jump of surprise and looked up at him. Her mouth opened but no sound came out as she looked from his face to his hips and back up again.

"I have very good cream," Rafe said, hoping to see her smile at him. "I would enjoy it if you ate—"

"I-I..." Jenna held up her hand. "Are you... unwell? I mean, do you need...mental help?"

Rafe didn't understand her question. He smiled at her, waiting for the dip of her eyes and the tiny giggle females on this planet made. She had such a pretty voice and an even prettier face. "I am Rafe and I do not require assistance at this moment."

Rafe slid into the booth across from her and reached into his bag to lift a white container. "I have chocolate, banana—"

"Oh, pie, you have cream pie," Jenna said, seeming to relax. "No. I don't eat pie."

"Ah, you eat parchment," he pushed at the pages on the table. They were filled with numbers and charts. Finally, she gave a small smile. The look

MICHELLE M. PILLOW

caused his heart to quicken and his stomach to tighten.

"I don't know what your game is, sitting down here, talking to me." Jenna gathered her papers and shoved them into her bag.

He glanced out the window, knowing he had to go just as soon as he had Princess Eve's food. Eve liked burgers to the point she threatened him if he came home empty-handed—well, not a real threat, but an almost real threat. "I have cheeseburgers. Would you like to eat that?"

"Do you have a food fetish? Is that what this is?" She shook her head. "I'm honestly not in the mood. I'm behind on paperwork for a thankless boss who is threatening layoffs because of the economy. The hot water in my shower is broken and my landlord is a deadbeat. And I lost my cat to old age. So, please, I don't need crazy right now. Just go be an alien with your girlfriends over there."

Rafe glanced over his shoulder. "Those girls are not my friends. You said you had not eaten today." Then seeing Barb placing his bag on the counter, he knew he didn't have much time. He hesitated. Something about Jenna made him want to stay.

"Barb, can I take mine to go, please?" Jenna asked loudly.

8

"Sure thing, hon." Barb disappeared into the back.

"Looks like your order is ready. You should pick it up now." Jenna gave a pointed look at the counter.

Rafe slowly stood and nodded. "As you so decree, m'lady."

2

Jenna Kearney watched the all-too-sexy man walk out of the diner. As gorgeous as he was to look at, she'd been burned by his kind before. The man was a foreign fitness model named Rafe for heaven's sake! His accent said he wasn't from the United States, and what else could he be with chiseled features, chin-length black hair, green eyes that seemed so bright they glowed? The tight black leather of his pants with the vest-shirt held together by crosslacing down the front and sides could only be high-end fashion. He was a magazine page come to life.

Men like that didn't go for girls like her. Period. She wasn't a fitness model. She didn't dress like a starlet. She liked talking about social policy and watching cute animal videos. Her idea of a hot night was reading a book and drinking a bottle of wine. Her cat, Ace, used to curl up next to her. Damn, she missed that cat. Knowing it had been his time didn't make it easier. Now she had no one to go home to. That's why she'd been coming to the diner at night to work.

Jenna put money on the counter, nodded her thanks, and took her grilled chicken sandwich to go. As she passed the table of women, she tried not to stare. They were what society called pretty—petite, caked in make-up and hair product, young and flirty. Jenna had never been like them. She had never been outgoing or the center of attention. In fact, she hated when all eyes in a room focused on her. It was the thing nightmares were made of. She took care of herself but not obsessively so. She read more than she socialized. She was...she was just plain Jenna.

The overhead bell jingled as she pushed through the door. She balanced her food bag while shoving her wallet into the messenger bag.

"You should come with me."

Jenna gasped, startled by the sound of Rafe's voice. She dropped her food into a puddle. For a confused moment, she stared at it. As if to protest, her stomach growled loudly. Under her breath, she muttered, "Dammit."

Rafe stepped out of the shadows. "I did not mean to frighten you. I was on my way to the portal when I realized I would not be coming back to this city again, at least not for an Earth year, and I did not want to risk you not being here. So I think you should come with me to my home."

Jenna frowned, glancing at the diner's front entrance. It was close enough she could run if she had to. "Portal? I think you mean airport terminal."

"So you will come?" Rafe smiled at her. The crazy guy did have a charming way about him. She would allow him that much.

"I don't know what you've heard about American girls, but we're not going to run off with strange men to foreign countries because of a cute accent, handsome face and some Hollywood induced notion of romance." Jenna relaxed when he did not act aggressively toward her. "I don't know why you picked me for your little game, but—"

"You like cats," he stated. "And you are very beautiful."

"Cats." Jenna gave a small laugh "You are a very strange man, sir."

"My name is Rafe. I am a prince."

"Oh, I don't have the patience for this." Jenna leaned over to pick up her ruined food. The bag dripped and she tossed it down the alley into a nearby dumpster. It was her fault for forgetting to eat, but knowing her plan to inhale a sandwich on her way home wasn't going to happen left her more than a little lightheaded. "Enjoy your flight home, Prince Rafe."

"I am not saying this right." His hand lifted as if to stop her from going back into the diner. "I find you very beautiful and when I saw you I felt what the dragons call a bonding connection start to form. You like cats so it must be a sign from the gods, and I wish to finger shackle you because I am a cat, and you will make a fine princess."

Jenna couldn't help herself. She started laughing. "English really is not your first language is it?"

"No," he answered. Rafe followed the acknowledgment with a series of strange sounds that could only be some obscure Scandinavian dialect.

When he finished, she said, "I think you're asking me on a date? But I'm not sure what dragons have to do with that. And I don't believe you are actually a cat."

"No, I am," he assured her.

"I think you mean you're a cat person."

"Yes. I am a cat person." He sighed and looked relieved that she understood. "And I promise to explain it better, but you must come with me now. I don't have a lot of time before the portal closes."

"Oh, ok, then," she said a little too dismissively. Lightheaded hunger was turning into grumpiness. "Don't want you to be late."

"Rafe," a man yelled before speaking very quickly in the same raspy language Rafe had used moments before. He appeared from down the street and walked purposefully toward them.

Rafe answered in kind, gesturing at Jenna and then at himself.

"Is he a cat person too?" Jenna asked, more to herself than to him.

"No, Finn is a dragon," Rafe said.

Jenna's patience was at an end. Food. Shower. Bed. That's what she needed. Not this crazy theatrical sideshow. Her heroes came in books, not real life. "Of course he is the dragon. And you're the cat. I would love to see that performance." She began to turn toward the diner to re-order. "But for now, I—"

"As you so decree, m'lady." Rafe's green eyes flashed with flecks of gold. His skin rippled, sprouting black fur over tanned flesh. His mouth changed, filling with fangs. He reached forward with hands that thickened and sprouted claws. A low sound started in the back of his throat.

Cat person.

Human cat.

Jenna's heart pounded wildly and for a moment she couldn't force her legs to move. Lightheadedness easily turned into dizzy hyperventilation. This entire situation couldn't be real. Stumbling back, she turned to run from the shape-shifter. A human dragon stood in front her. Brown flesh formed a shell over the dragon's body, protruding from his forehead to frame golden eyes. She gasped in panic.

"Drag...drag..." She tried to speak.

"We are draqueens," the dragon said, his tone harsher than before.

In an effort to get away, Jenna caught her foot on a sidewalk crack. The dragon reached for her and grabbed her wrist. She jerked violently out of his reach.

"Jenna," Rafe said, seconds before hands touched her from behind. She jerked again in the other direction, losing her footing as she stumbled. Her head struck a metal streetlight with a reverberating *clang* and in the seconds following she felt herself plummeting into blackness.

3

Rafe stared at Prince Finn in shock. They held Jenna awkwardly as her body dangled just inches from hitting the sidewalk. Finn slid his arm behind Jenna's back to lift her to a better position. The men stood, holding her between them.

"Did we break her?" Finn asked, glancing around. "What just happened?"

"She said she wanted to see the shift," Rafe answered. "She likes cats, so it must have been you that scared her."

"You told me to shift for her," Finn said, clearly not willing to take the blame. "Are we in trouble here? The elders can't find out we shifted on Earth. They'd never let us come back. Should we put her somewhere?" The dragon prince leaned over, looking at a small passage between the two buildings. It smelled like garbage. "We have to go. I don't want to remain trapped on Earth. Our parents will never forgive us if we don't return, and the people will panic. Not to mention your brother will probably kill us for sure this time."

"I can handle Ivar," Rafe said, not terribly worried about his older brother.

Every place that he touched Jenna tingled. The smell of her hair teased his senses. Her lips parted slightly and he had the strongest desire to kiss her. He wouldn't, of course, not without her active participation, but the urge was very real. "I'm not leaving her here."

"Then where? We have to leave her somewhere safe. Do you wish to prop her against the door where her people will find her?"

"I'm not leaving her *at all*," Rafe clarified. "This is my wife, Jenna."

"Did she agree?" Finn appeared doubtful. "I mean, does she know? It didn't look like you talked to her for very long. I won't kidnap a woman. Eve has told us that we don't always understand Earth ways. Women do not wish to be kidnaped, even if we are royalty."

"We met when I was getting Princess Eve's food. I told her I wished to be with her, and she said 'oh, ok, then,' which Eve said ok means yes. So she is willing," Rafe answered. "The gods were every clear. She told me she likes cats. I saw her and, well, your brother will understand." He paused a little dismissingly. An unmated man surely couldn't know what he did now. "Prince Kyran has mated. He will understand what I mean."

"I can't understand, but you know all because you have been mated for three seconds?" Finn arched a brow. "Are you serious? Just this evening you were telling me that you were going to delay that final moment and enjoy our trips through the portal. In fact, I believe you wagered me that you would be the last prince to marry."

Rafe grimaced. "Oh, yeah, I forgot about the wager."

"You can bet I'm collecting on it." Finn shifted Jenna's weight away from Rafe. "If you reached an agreement with her, then let's go. I'll carry her so you don't get distracted gazing all lovesick at her like that." Finn nodded to where Rafe had set the food bags down. "Fetch Eve's food."

"Definitely don't want to forget that," Rafe agreed as he grabbed the bags. He also took the satchel Jenna had dropped. Though he wanted to keep holding his woman, Finn was probably right. If he did, he'd never make it back to the portal. Even now, it felt like she was in his arms. In that one touch, he'd known everything he needed to know.

"Eve may not be a dragon-shifter, but I'm sure that one can breathe fire when she's upset," Finn said.

"A fitting future queen." Rafe grinned at Jenna. "I think my Jenna will make a fine Var princess."

"We better run." Finn led the way home.

The portal was hidden from view on the Earth side and only those who knew where it was could find it. The sound of cars speeding over a big roadway greeted them as they hurried under an overpass. The manmade hill leading to the underside of the bridge was steep, and it became too short to stand near the top.

"Where were you?" Prince Ivar demanded. He didn't sound pleased, but then that was hardly new. Rafe's brother never sounded very happy. "The portal is about to cl—*what is she?*"

"She is a Jenna," Finn answered, stopping on the incline. "Here, take her through the portal."

Ivar grimaced, even as he reached for her. He

cradled her into his lap and then pushed forcibly back into the concrete footing. He disappeared into the portal, taking Jenna with him.

Finn waited a few seconds before diving forward after Ivar. Rafe cradled the food against his chest and fell more than jumped into the invisible barrier. The trip itself had no feeling, but afterward, as he was spit out on the other side, his entire body tingled as if tiny knives stabbed his skin. It wasn't painful, just unpleasant, and it kept him immobile for a moment.

"Get your *gbwor* off me, Finn," Ivar yelled. The sound was followed by a series of *thwaps* and Finn's laughter. "Ow. Stop that, woman."

The soft purple glow of the portal lit the black stone of the cave. Dragons and cats were carved into the stone chamber, leading away from the portal. They were symbolic of the shifters' exodus from Earth long ago. Jagged rocks littered the floor from when their ancestors had caved in the chamber after they first arrived on Qurilixen. The portal light was weak, a sign that it would close soon. The passageway leading out of the caves into the valley was open, and a cool breeze made its way into them. Rafe took a deep breath, shaking off the aftereffects.

Jenna swung an old staff at Ivar, hitting him

across the back. Rafe's brother did not defend himself. "I'm leaving and you can't stop me."

"Fine," Ivar growled. He grabbed the shaft mid-swing, tore it from her fingers and tossed it aside. Then, in a swift move he had her pinned to his chest. Jenna kicked and thrashed violently, trying to get free from her captor. Ivar took her blows, not hurting her. "Out of the way, Rafe. I'm tossing this one back. Finn does not seem to want her anymore now that she is awake."

"Unhand her," Rafe demanded, springing into action. The portal glow faded by small degrees.

"Let me go!" Jenna demanded.

"What is it to you, Rafe?" Ivar asked, clearly confused.

"She is my wife," Rafe said. He lifted his hands as if to accept Jenna into his arms. "And she said she wanted to be with me."

"You?" Ivar said doubtfully. "Stop playing games. Let me push her back to Earth. She's clearly not suited for our world. I will not be a part of your immature rebellions. If you will not take marriage seriously, then you have no business joining us on our trips. I will not let you have Finn's discarded bride."

Jenna thrashed against Ivar's hold.

"It is no joke, brother. She is my mate. If you push her through that portal, I will leave with her, and you will have to explain why I didn't come back with you to our parents. Where she goes, I go. We have something you cannot understand."

4

JENNA DIDN'T KNOW what the strange men were saying in their gruff and growly voices. All she knew is that one minute she was on the streets of Kansas City and the next she was in some mammoth guy's arms in a cave beside a giant swirling purple light being welcomed to the planet of Qurilixen.

Planet.

Of Qurilixen.

What the hell?

Rafe stood with open arms, smiling at her. She kicked harder, only to stumble in surprise when the giant man abruptly let her go. Jenna brought her joined hands up and hit the big guy across the side of the head. He looked stunned at the attack.

"Touch me, and I'll kill you," Jenna warned. The

purple light faded, casting shadows over the cave as a softer light came in from an unseen source. Adrenaline filled her veins, and she tensed, ready to mount another attack.

"She has fire," a man said. She stiffened as she understood him. "Well chosen, Rafe."

"Quiet, Finn," the big guy answered.

"Well, she does," Finn mumbled. If she wasn't mistaken, it sounded like the man laughed. "Queen Lassairfhina will like her."

"Jenna likes cats," Rafe said. Suddenly, she remembered what had scared her so badly that she'd run into a pole and knocked herself unconscious.

"Cat-shifter," she managed weakly. "And man dragon."

"We are called Draig," Finn corrected. "Not man dragon."

"We are Var," Rafe said. "And you are correct. We are cat-shifters."

With the last of the purple vortex fading away, darkness loomed all around. A softer light crept through the opposite side of the cave. Facial features became shadowed mysteries. The fear inside her grew. Her heart pounded hard. The men didn't move.

"Don't touch me," Jenna warned.

"No one is touching you," Rafe said. He sounded confused. Or was it concerned? "Do you feel like you are being touched?"

"What are you going to do?" Her head throbbed and she gingerly fingered the large bump that had formed beneath her hair.

"We should greet the Draig elders," the big man said. "They will be waiting for us."

"What are you going to do *with me*?" Jenna insisted.

"We are going to bring you to meet the elders." Rafe enunciated his words as if that would make her understand. Then to the big man, he said, "I think your accent is too thick, brother. You should pronounce your words better."

"Why did you bring me here?" Jenna edged away from them toward where she had witnessed Rafe appearing out of the purple light. She felt along an engraved stone. Finding a loose rock, she grabbed it with a shaking hand. She focused her attention on the shaded outline of the big man who'd restrained her. Her arm twitched as she tried to decide how best to defend herself. "What do you want?"

Rafe's brother moved, and she threw the rock at him. A shadowed hand shot out and caught the rock with seemingly little effort. "You are right, Finn, she does have fire." He chuckled. "But very bad aim."

"Leave her be, Ivar," Rafe told his brother.

Ivar dropped the rock and turned toward the small stream of light coming into the cave. "Take a moment with her before we begin the journey home."

Finn walked with Ivar out of the chamber.

"What are you going to do?" Jenna continued to feel the wall, looking for a lever or a button, anything that would activate the portal so she could go home.

"Do you not understand?" Rafe asked.

Her head ached where she had struck it on the pole. Abandoning her search for a portal switch, Jenna pressed her hand to her temple. "Something's not right. I need to go back." She pushed to her feet, swaying as she stumbled toward the inert portal. Her vision blurred as she tried to see in the dim light. "I need a doctor."

Jenna felt her body move by an outside force. The world spun violently but then she found herself in Rafe's arms. "I didn't know you were ill. Forgive me."

"What are you going to do?" she whispered. Her body jostled as he ran with her. Jenna closed her eyes tight, unable to take the motion. "What are you going to do?"

5

"WHAT IS WRONG WITH HER?" Rafe stared at Princess Eve, willing her to help her fellow human.

Hazel eyes stared back at him like he was insane. When he had first met Eve, she'd had a blue streak in her brown hair and had been screaming songs on a stage to angry dancers. Though the blue was gone, the wildness it represented was not. It was there in her eyes and in her wry tone.

"What's wrong with her? For one, she's not hard-headed like the rest of you." Eve turned her attention back to the unconscious Jenna and carefully cleaned the large knot that had formed in the woman's hair-line before dropping the rag into the water basin next to the bed.

Rafe swallowed nervously. "Fix her. She's my mate, and I don't like her like this."

Eve arched a brow. For a moment, he thought she was going to say something about his demanding tone, but then seemed to think better about it. "What happened?"

"She fell into a column," Rafe said. "The portal was closing and there wasn't much time, so we carried her through."

"Was she awake when you carried her through?" Eve asked.

Rafe shook his head in denial. "No, but she woke up after we came through the portal and threw a rock at my brother and then fell asleep again. I know what you're going to ask. She does want to be my wife. The gods' signs were clear." He gave a small smile. "She likes cats."

"Actually, I was going to ask if she vomited, complained of a headache, dizziness, seemed confused?" Eve pulled open one of Jenna's lids and then let it close.

Rafe's stomach tightened in worry at Eve's tone. "She kept repeating the same question. And she stumbled as she asked for a doctor."

"I'm guessing she has a concussion," Eve said, pressing on the wound. Jenna moaned and opened her eyes. "Ah, there she is. Hello, Jenna. I'm Eve. Looks like you've bumped your head."

Jenna furrowed her brow. Her eyes moved from Eve to Rafe. "Is this a hospital?"

Eve glanced around the Draig marriage tent. The servants set it up every time the dragon princes went through the portal in hopes that Finn would need it to finish the dragon marriage ritual. Rafe's people were much simpler in their mating process. The bond happened naturally and only took the will of two people, not endless formalities.

"I think you might have a concussion. I am no doctor, but I am pretty sure we should keep you awake until that swelling goes down," Eve said.

Jenna's dazed eyes stared at Rafe, and she touched the bump on her head. There was so much he wanted to say to her, but now was not the time.

"You are beautiful," he told her.

Jenna frowned, her eyes focusing in on him and becoming clearer.

"Ok, there, lover boy, why don't you wait outside?" Eve gave him a push toward the tent flap.

Rafe resisted. "I cannot leave her."

"I need you to find me something very cold to put on her head and the palace doctor." Eve pushed harder, trying to force him to go.

He stared at the tent flap, not wanting to leave his woman. "Ivar already went for a doctor."

"Seriously, Rafe?" Eve pushed harder. "Go. Now. I'll come find you when she's ready."

JENNA WATCHED the slender Eve push the much larger Rafe out of the tent before turning back to her. Rafe still wore the high fashion clothing, but Eve looked like she'd just come from a hippie pajama party with loose pants and a tunic shirt. Her brown hair was pulled up at the sides to create a braided circlet around the back of her head.

Eve held up her hands, half in ready defense and half in concern. "You're not going to scream, are you? Or freak out? You look like you might scream and freak out."

Jenna slowly sat up and felt the room spin. "I'm not sure I'm up to freaking out at the moment."

"Because if you wanted to scream and freak out I wouldn't blame you. That's what I did when I woke up here." Eve gestured around the tent. "I don't suppose you're just hung over? I was hung over. I don't remember the journey across that first time either, so I know that it can be a little disorientating to wake up here."

"No, not hung over." Eve gingerly fingered the bump on her head. Her hair around the wound was damp, but it felt like the swelling had gone down. She glanced at her hand to make sure it wasn't blood. The wound had been cleaned, evidenced by the pink-stained rag floating in a bowl of water.

The sounds of nature invaded the red pyramid shaped tent from outside. The walls were illuminated to attest to the daytime and the thin material moved with the breeze. A furry rug spread over the ground. Jenna sat on a large bed in the center. "Is this your home?"

Eve laughed, but Jenna didn't get the joke. "No. It's just a tent."

Jenna continued to stare at her surroundings. Her body ached. Her empty stomach hated her. Her lightheaded brain refused to concentrate.

"You passed out." Eve sat down on the edge of the bed. "Twice from what I understand. Like I said, you might have a concussion."

"Low blood sugar. I just need food." Jenna didn't feel like she was in immediate danger, but then she wasn't exactly thinking clearly. "Where am I?"

"These men," Eve mumbled to herself and gave a

long sigh. She went to the table and lifted a generic plastic bag the diner used for takeout orders. "We'll take things slowly since apparently the situation wasn't explained fully. The burgers might not be hot, but you're welcome to them."

"Oh, thank you, thank you, thank you," Jenna said as she reached to take the bag. At this point, she would have eaten just about anything. Unable to help the moan that escaped her, she took a bite and then another. Once her mouth tasted food, she was unable to stop until she'd consumed the burger and was half way through a second one.

"Better?" Eve asked.

Her mouth full, Jenna nodded and then shook her head in denial.

"You want to freak out now?" Eve stood.

Jenna nodded. She swallowed. The food went down hard. Setting the rest of the second burger down, she asked in a rush, "What is this all about? What's happening? Why me? Why—"

"Ok, ok." Eve stood. "First, you need to know no one will hurt you. Second, you're not crazy." She held out her hand. "Come outside with me."

Jenna didn't take the woman's hand but stood to follow. With each passing moment her body felt better, and her mind began to panic. Not waiting for

Eve to make it through the door to the tent, she pushed past her and ran outside. The light appeared green, perhaps foretelling an upcoming storm. Why else would it be tinted so strangely?

Jenna glanced around. They were in the woods. The tree bark had a strange bubbling texture as if they'd been heated up in the centers and their skin boiled into hard scabs. Yellow ferns covered the ground as if starved of sunlight.

"Am I dead?" Jenna whispered, not comprehending what she was seeing. "Is this...purgatory?"

"You're on Qurilixen. It's a planet," Eve explained. "There's a portal between Earth and this world. Kind of like an intergalactic escalator."

"Wait. That's what the big man said. He welcomed me to the planet of Qurilixen. Cats and dragons and aliens and..." Jenna eyed Eve. "What are you?"

"Human. From Earth."

"Why are we here?" Jenna slowly reached to touch a tree as if to assure herself it was real. The rough texture caught against her fingers.

"I'm here because this is my husband's home. You're here because..."

At Eve's hesitation, Jenna dropped her hand and studied the woman's face. "Because?"

"Because Rafe wants to…"

"Want's to?" Jenna prompted.

"He wants to marry you."

"Marry me?" Jenna did the only thing she could. She laughed. The sexy foreign model alien guy wanted to marry her? On no plain of reality did that make sense.

"I know it sounds bad, but really, it's not. It's hard to explain. They're not like us, I mean like humans. They're, ah…" Eve frowned. "Ok, so they're a little crazy by our standards when it comes to courtship. See this planet doesn't have a lot of women because of low female birth rates, so they travel to Earth to look for love. I swear it's not as hokey as it sounds. I mean, wow, this is harder to explain than I thought it would be."

"Are you telling me I'm on an intergalactic date?" Jenna had always believed in the probability of aliens. It had always felt too vain to believe humans were the only intelligent life in the infinite unknown. That said, she never thought she'd be making contact with them.

"That's an astute way of putting it," Eve said.

"I don't date." Jenna had other concerns. Job. Rent. Retirement account. She gasped. "My bag. I had papers for work that I need to finish. My wallet was in there. My keys."

"You're on an alien planet and you're worried about work?"

"Well, I..." Jenna made a weak noise and again touched the tree bark. "I think my vision is messed up. I see green."

"You'll get used to it. The planet has three suns. One of them is blue, so the light is different than what you're used to."

"Oh." Jenna nodded.

"I get it. Your brain is swirling with thoughts and—"

"Ivar has brought doctors who know humans." Rafe crashed through the brush. His eyes met hers and he smiled. Jenna had to give it to the man. He was naturally charming without even trying. She forced herself to look away. He continued, "We are very lucky they are visiting the palaces."

"It is the will of the gods," Ivar said, following his brother. Both cat-shifters wore tighter pants and shirts with cross laces down the center of their chests. The lacing exposed a sexy river of flesh from muscular stomachs to strong necks.

Jenna looked at the gruff Ivar in the light of day. His

eyes matched Rafe's, the same shade of bright green, but his hair was lighter and his expression less open. When he looked directly at her, she had the impression he didn't appreciate his brother's choice of potential brides.

The sound of movement came from behind the two men. Feet shuffled on the forest floor punctuated by a rapid clicking. All attention turned to the noise.

"My ladies," Rafe said as two thin gray beings appeared behind him. "These are our guests."

"Little gray men," Eve whispered before Jenna had a chance to process what she was seeing.

The beings stood about four feet high topped with heads double the size of a human skull. Large glassy black eyes focused their attention to the women. Their noses, ears and mouths were little more than slits in the taut stretch of their dark gray skin. Flesh appeared to have a plastic sheen. Skintight lighter gray jumpsuits covered their bodies, giving way to the sexless shape of their humanoid forms. Mouth and nose holes twitched as they clicked to each other.

"They're real?" Jenna asked. Every crazy abduction story that had ever been laughed at was possibly true?

"They're Reticulans." Ivar gestured that she should go back into the tent. "M'lady, if you please."

Jenna did not please.

The slightly taller of the two gray aliens shuffled toward her. She stiffened as he lifted his finger to touch her forehead. The tip of his long, skinny finger was freezing against her. She watched his black eyes flash with a pearl sheen.

"Human. Earth." The alien withdrew his finger and clicked to his friend.

"Did you fix my head?" Jenna reached to touch the bump. It was still there, and she didn't feel any differently.

"You will call me Roswell," the first alien said in English. Roswell went to push his finger to his partner's head.

"Human. Earth." The second alien came forward and reached behind his back to pull out a small hand-held device. "We can fix human Earth. You will call me Mogul."

"As in the famous UFO incident in Roswell, New Mexico and Project Mogul?" Eve asked.

The aliens began to click louder and faster. It sounded like they were laughing.

"We have not done missionary work for human Earth for a long while," Roswell said.

"Probing." Mogul lifted his device and came at her.

"What is that thing?" Jenna backed away from them, not wanting the aliens to probe her. She looked at Rafe to see if he'd intervene.

"We fix one..." Mogul paused and looked at Roswell.

"Colon. We fix one infected colon," Roswell said.

"And suddenly every human Earth wishes for us to probe their colon for no medical reason. We find it a very strange request so we leave to cure other planets. Human Earth is not invited to be part of the Medical Alliance for Planetary Health. They are not ready." Mogul's eyes glossed over. "We will not probe you, human Earth."

"Very glad to hear it," Jenna said. "I don't want you to probe me."

Mogul lifted his device and pressed it to Jenna's head. She flinched but instantly felt warmth spreading from her forehead to her temple to behind her eye. The tingling cured the dull ache. When she touched her head, the bump had disappeared.

"A fine demonstration," Ivar said. "We will discuss trade for your device."

Ivar leaned over. Roswell touched the cat-shifter's forehead and then reached to press his finger to Mogul's. The two aliens began speaking in the gruff native Qurilixian language.

"Ah, thank you," Jenna said belatedly.

The aliens paused, turning to her. Rafe said something to them in his native tongue. The aliens answered in kind.

"You are welcome," Rafe translated.

"But, they..." Jenna was confused.

"They only hold one extra language in their brains at a time. Right now, they are speaking to Ivar about procuring more of those medical devices for our fragile humans." Rafe smiled like it was a compliment. "Do you feel better now?"

"Ha! Did you hear that?" Eve bumped Jenna's shoulder. "There is such a thing as alien probing."

"I have accounting and office management degrees," Jenna announced.

Eve and Rafe appeared confused.

"I work in an office with spreadsheets and numbers." She stared at Rafe and frowned. "I like my own company and books and daydreaming about things I'll never do. I make logical decisions." Gesturing after the aliens, she said, "This isn't logical. I'm going to find that portal and go home."

6

RAFE WATCHED Jenna walk into the forest away from them. He frowned at Eve. "What did you do to my wife?"

Eve placed her hands on her hips. "What did *I* do?"

"She was fine until I left her alone with you." Rafe motioned to his bride. He kept an ear on her, listening to the sound of her footfall in the forest. "She's not even going in the right direction."

Eve marched over to Rafe and poked him in the chest. "You should have paid attention when I told you about Earth women. You can't just snatch and grab and kidnap what you want. If she is unhappy, that is on you. If she gets hurt in any way, that's going to be me kicking your ass, cat. Got it?"

"I believe you would." Rafe didn't dare lay his hand on a woman even in defense, so he let Eve poke at him.

"I'm serious, Rafe. I agreed to help you guys only because it would keep you from bumbling around and kidnapping my people."

He gave her a small smile. "They keep telling us that Earth woman are fragile, but you, princess, are as tough as any shifter female I have ever known."

Eve waved her hand dismissingly. "Ah, save your charm for Jenna. You're lucky I know your intentions are honorable. And go after her before she gets eaten by a yorkin."

"Yorkins stay higher in the mountains," Rafe said as he went to follow Jenna. For some reason, he let her walk, easily tracking her as she moved through the forest. It wasn't much of a hunt, but he still found himself smiling as he pursued her. He wanted her, terribly. That wasn't surprising. She was made for him.

"Which way to the portal?" Jenna stood on the path facing him. Apparently he had not tracked her quietly enough.

Rafe pointed behind him toward the cave. He liked the way the wind stirred her hair around her shoulders. She still wore the Earth clothes, the material stained with dirt from the cave floor. It didn't matter. She looked like a princess to him.

"Show me. I want to go home." She motioned that he should lead the way.

"I'm sorry. I can't do that." He didn't move. "The portal won't take you home for about an Earth year."

Her mouth opened, and she stared at him. A small sound left her, but she didn't speak. Mesmerized by her lips, Rafe tilted forward to kiss her.

Jenna leaned back, not letting him. "What do you think you are doing?"

"I wish to kiss you now." He again moved to claim her mouth with his.

Jenna stepped back. "I'm pretty sure Stockholm syndrome takes more than a few hours to set in."

"What is this Stockholm?" Rafe asked. His heart was beating fast, maybe too fast. Her reluctance only made him want to kiss her more. He did not mind being teased with anticipation.

"A psychological disorder when kidnap victims fall in love with their captor." Jenna walked past him and began to make her way back toward the Draig marriage tent.

"You mean to say you need a few hours to fall in

love with me?" Rafe's smile faded. "Wait, where are you going?"

"To find Eve. She is the only person here who seems to make any sense." Jenna walked faster.

This time as he followed her, he frowned. "But, what about being my wife?"

7

JENNA HAD no idea what she was doing. When Rafe tried to kiss her, she'd wanted him to. Instinct pulled her away from him. Or maybe it was fear. As much as she was the confident woman in most areas of her life, when it came to men she didn't have a lot of practice. When it came to incredible sex-god men, she had absolutely no experience.

A man like Rafe would have to have practice, even on a planet in need of women. He had so much sexual confidence it virtually radiated off of him. His body was like a magnet, luring women to touch, to kiss, to...

"You have stopped walking. Did you change your mind?"

Jenna stiffened to hear the low tone of his voice. "I have no idea what I'm doing."

"Are you confused again? Do I need to find Roswell?" Rafe was instantly at her side. Before she knew what he was doing, he had her lifted in his arms and was jogging through the forest with her.

"Ah," she cried in surprise. "I'm not injured. Put me down."

He slowed to a walk. "You're not still injured?"

"No, I'm just," she struggled for words. His body radiated heat into hers. "I'm on an alien planet."

He kept walking. His voice dipped. "Yes. You are."

A shiver ran up her spine. "Put me down."

"I don't want to." He grinned and changed direction.

"Where are we going now?" Jenna didn't struggle as much as she should have.

"You have two choices. I can take you to Princess Eve where you will be expected to present yourself to the royal Draig family. Normally, this would happen when a new bride comes out of the portal. You will be excused because you were injured unless you want the introduction. Or, I can take you to my home."

Jenna stiffened. "Could you, just...? Put me down, please."

Rafe obeyed.

"I can't marry you. I don't know you. You don't know me." She put distance between them, using the uneven forest floor as an excuse not to look at him as she navigated over it. "I can only take one crazy thing at a time. Being stuck on an alien world with no work, no home, no idea what I'm doing is about all the crazy I can handle."

"As my wife you do not need to work."

"Am I being lost in translation?" Jenna threw her hands to the side in frustration. "I'm not your wife. We are not getting married. I have a few more serious things to consider right now than dating."

"But...you like cats and I am a cat person." He said it like that one simple fact should completely change her mind.

"I also like to eat and sleep indoors and pay my bills," she countered. "Well, ok, so I don't like paying my bills but I like knowing I can afford to."

"I don't know what bills are, but we only have to camp outside if we do not make it past the borderlands before you tire. And I will feed you. Are you hungry? I will find you food." He tried to touch her.

"Rafe, stop," Jenna ordered. "I'm sure you mean

well, but nothing you do will change the fact you brought me here without my consent."

"I have heard enough."

Jenna gasped and turned to see Ivar leaning against a nearby tree. She had not heard his approach. He held her messenger bag over one shoulder.

"Ivar, this is none of your concern," Rafe said in irritation.

Ivar ignored him. "M'lady, on behalf of my people, I apologize for this misunderstanding." Ivar came before her and bowed his head. "I would not have allowed your travel had I known your reluctance to marry my brother. I cannot undo what has been done, but I can assure you that you will be treated with all the respect and protection as would have been given my sister until you agree to marry. No one will harm you, and you will not be made to mate unless you choose."

Jenna didn't want to think about marriage. Considering her options, there was only one choice—take Ivar's offer of protection. How else would she eat or live for the next year on an alien world? She nodded weakly.

"It is settled. Lady Jenna is under my protection."

Ivar motioned that she should go with him. "Have you any needs?"

"No. Not at the moment." Jenna glanced at Rafe. His eyes pleaded with her to change her mind.

"Rafe, take our leave of the Draig family and procure supplies for the trip then catch up to us. We head for the borderlands." Ivar turned his back on his brother and lifted his arm toward her. "M'lady, please, come." Though the words were polite, everything the man said sounded like a command. "Allow me to escort you to your new home."

8

Rafe glared at his brother's back. He wanted nothing more than to deny Ivar's claim of protection and take Jenna back. Unfortunately, Ivar was the oldest and as future Var king the only people who could reverse his claim on Jenna was their parents, or Ivar himself which would never happen. Rafe had never wished that he'd been born first until now.

They'd traveled in silence. Though it would have been easier to run over the countryside in shifted form, they instead rode ceffyls down the side of the mountain. The dragons bred the ugly beasts and seemed to have an affinity for the creatures. Perhaps it was the reptilian eyes and cumbersome bodies that reminded them of their dragon ancestors. Rafe tried to suppress a small laugh at the thought as he reached to tap the center horn on the creatures head to redirect its course.

He waited for those moments when Jenna would look in his direction. It didn't happen too often. She occasionally whispered under her breath about them expecting her to ride a rhinoceros lizard, then about there being three suns, and several reassurances that she wasn't crazy.

Mountain paths led down a valley. The gray earth became streaked with light red, only to darken as they finally made it to the level ground of the borderlands. The red earth wasn't the only thing to change. Trees grew wider here, the trucks so thick people could carve homes out of the older ones—not that anyone tried. The large leaves stretched wide, reaching for the suns to form canopies.

The smell of the marshes gave the first true hint of home. Rafe had spent many nights running through the forest surrounding the Var palace. Moss clung to branches, thin curtains to obscure the vision. The woods were quiet but for the hum of insects. If he stretched his shifter hearing over the distance, he detected the sound of cats running through fallen leaves. He heard laughter, a mother at her Var children, children playing with each other, a family. The sound captured his attention and held it. Family.

Children. He'd been so busy having fun he'd never thought about children, at least not beyond his parents' lectures about responsibility.

"We stop here for the night," Ivar announced in their native language. "She looks as if she might fall off her mount."

Rafe blinked, bringing his thoughts back to his traveling party. They'd arrived at an old way station. There were several such places on Var land, built as shelters for those feral-living cat-shifters roaming the countryside without a home. The planet did not have many storms, but when they did they were hard and fierce.

Rafe dismounted and went toward Jenna. Ivar made it to her first, offering his hand to help her to the ground. She took the assistance but then stepped away from them.

"You have a lovely home," Jenna said.

Rafe couldn't help his small laugh. Ivar narrowed his eyes at him to make him stop.

"It is a way station," Ivar said. "We will rest here for the night."

"Will it be night soon?" Jenna looked up at the sky.

"It is late evening now," Rafe explained. "We do not have darkness like you are accustomed to each night." He pointed up. "The suns keep it light, but the color shifts to keep the hours."

She looked at her hand as if studying the light.

"I found your world just as wondrous," he offered, hoping to draw her into a conversation."

"Build a fire," Ivar ordered gruffly with a curt nod of his head that Rafe should gather wood. He motioned that Jenna should go inside the station.

Rafe glared at his brother in warning. His felt the shift threaten his entire being. Jenna was his. His. Ivar had no right to interfere.

Ivar's eyes flashed with gold. Now was not the time to fight, and they both knew it. Rafe growled and backed away to do as he was told.

Though he trusted his brother, Rafe couldn't help listening to Jenna move around inside the way station cabin to make sure she was safe. He gathered wood to build a fire. The way stations were safe havens, but they lacked some of the more refined luxuries of their palace home. It was not where he wanted to spend the night with his bride. For, regardless of what anyone said, Jenna would be his wife. Each second brought with it a deeper surety. He felt that truth as indisputably as the wood in his hands.

"I'm not sending her back," Rafe said before

turning to face Ivar. His brother leaned against a tree, watching him. "And I won't let you send her away."

"I have no intention of letting her go back to Earth. What is done will remain done. We cannot risk her telling others about us. The gods allowed her through the portal, so it is her fate to be here." Ivar frowned. "Do not turn those eyes to me, brother. She is not my future, and I will not force her into one. She is free to choose her Var path."

"I am her path," Rafe asserted.

Ivar gave a small disbelieving laugh and shook his head. "Are you listening to yourself? What makes you think you're ready for such a blessing? You mock our sacred traditions. You try to seduce the priest-esses. You try to seduce every human woman who will look in your direction without any thought of marriage until tonight. You laugh and play through life and do not attempt to humble yourself before the gods. What makes you think you're worthy of a wife, no matter how badly you want her? Lady Jenna deserves what every woman deserves—a husband worthy of her heart."

"I do not disrespect our gods." Rafe's breathing deepened. He wanted to force his hands over his brother's mouth and silence him. The words stung and he didn't want to admit there was any truth to what Ivar said.

"I did not say you disrespect them. I said you do not humble yourself. You dance through life—"

"And you take life too seriously," Rafe charged. "If you haven't noticed this isn't the old days. We're not constantly at battle. There is no need for me to go command the armies. I keep the men trained. I do my duty."

Ivar's eyes flashed. "How can you not feel the weight of our people on your head?"

"Maybe because I'm not meant to be king," Rafe countered.

"So you oversee a few tournaments and keep the men trained? You do only that which you are required to do, no more. You are a child." Ivar pointed toward the cabin. "Lady Jenna deserves a man willing to work for her. You want her? Earn her. Prove you are worthy of her, brother. Don't run from the challenge because it does not come easy."

"Prove myself to her or to you as her guardian?" Rafe tightly gripped the wood he carried. "What would you have me do to win the bride the gods already gave me?"

Ivar gestured to the wood. "You can start by building her a fire."

9

Jenna was thankful for the stretched canvas bed in the corner of the dusty log cabin. The planked walls were cut from the large trees outside, the texture rough as if they'd been sawed by hand rather than machine. The ground appeared to be the base of that tree, a smoothed, polished stump turned into a floor.

She burrowed under the thick woven blanket, not caring that it had a slight musk. The physical exercise of riding the rhino lizard combined with the all-too-confusing emotional stress of finding herself on an alien planet made sleep sound like the idea of the century. Her eyes closed and for the moment she didn't care about anything beyond the darkness.

A tickling sensation moved over her forehead.

Jenna gasped, coming out of the sleepy haze. It took her a moment to remember where she was and why.

Rafe sat next to her, his fingers retreating from where he'd brushed the hair from her face. She automatically rubbed the spot where he touched her and pulled to the side so she could sit up without bumping into him. The room smelled of campfire, but the fire had been lit and then snuffed in the fireplace. All that remained were tiny glowing embers.

"I was worried when you did not wake up," he said. "You slept for many hours."

Jenna couldn't meet his gaze. There was warmth in his voice, the sound drawing her in with its natural charm. Heat radiated from his body like a beacon, calling her to him.

"You're like the pied piper of sex appeal," she muttered to herself.

He grinned. She frowned.

"I know sex, but what is the pied piper?" He fingered a strand of her hair. "I should like to see the appeal of this kind of sex."

Jenna made a weak noise, completely speechless. Subtle clearly wasn't in Rafe's DNA. Rafe took advantage of her stunned state and kissed her. She inhaled sharply against his mouth. The surprised sound didn't stop him. Though, to be fair, neither did she. Instead, she sat frozen, shocked by the way his lips moved confidently against hers. Everything about him was a seduction—his heat, his touch, his voice, those damned confident eyes.

"I don't you do," she whispered when he pulled away ever so slightly. "I mean I don't do you." He drew back another inch. "I mean I don't want to do you—ugh, I don't want you to get the wrong idea when we do, or think we're going to do..."

Time to shut up, Jenna.

Jenna obeyed the little voice inside her head, for apparently the big voice inside her throat was babbling nonsense and making her look like an inarticulate fool.

"So no pied piper?" He looked a little disappointed.

Jenna shook her head in denial.

"Will you at least explain it to me?" He sounded very hopeful.

She shook her head in harder denial.

"I am fine with regular sex." He leaned in for another kiss. "I would like to pleasure you now."

Jenna didn't have the forethought to artfully avoid his mouth. Luckily, or maybe not so luckily, she didn't have to.

"Rafe!" Ivar barked from the doorway. "Unhand

my ward. She is to be treated like a solarflower under my protection so keep your clumsy paws to yourself. There will be no plucking of her beauty."

Did Ivar just call her a fragile, delicate flower?

"Allow her to make her choice," Rafe countered as he stood. "Tell him you wish to be my bride."

It took her a moment to realize Rafe was looking at her expectantly.

"Lady Jenna?" Ivar asked.

"I, uh..." Jenna slowly stood. "I'm hungry. And, um, weren't we supposed to walk again today?"

"I brought you food." Ivar handed her a very large bundle. "It is not much, but tonight we will feast."

Jenna peeked inside the cloth and found pea-sized orange berries. Curious, she sniffed them. They didn't give off much of a smell. With both brothers staring at her, she didn't have much of a choice but to place one in her mouth. The firm fruit popped when she bit into it, filling her mouth with the taste of peaches and mint. She gave the brothers a small smile, and they relaxed.

"I paid a few of the borderland farmers to return the ceffyls to the Draig. Come. We walk the rest of the way." Ivar led them from the way station.

Rafe reached over and took some of the fruit. He whispered, "You are worth the chase, m'lady," before winking and tossing the pieces into his mouth.

10

SLEEP HAD DONE MUCH to clear her thinking—at least now that Rafe wasn't kissing her. So much had happened in such a short time and the way she saw it she had two choices. She could whine and cry and plead to go home, or she could see this for the opportunity that it was.

Home was safe and familiar, but that is all it was. She had no one waiting for her at the end of the day. She hated her boss. She hated her building manager. She hated her leaky small apartment. Her mother had died. Her father was out of the picture. She had work friends, but no one who would report her missing or even notice beyond the annoying fact they were reassigned her unfinished workload.

This new world was exciting. Apparently, Rafe

thought her kissable. Ivar wanted to take care of her and practically demanded she live under his protection until she figured out what she wanted to do. No one tried to harm her—she could hardly blame Rafe because she ran herself into a pole. The air was fresh. She had the opportunity to meet real life little gray men—*freaking real live aliens!* Jenna glanced at Rafe. Well, these Var and Draig men were aliens, too, but little gray men were like alien-aliens. People waited their whole lives for even half of the adventure she was currently on.

The brothers had been leading her through the woods in silence. The trees reminded her of redwoods, towering so high she couldn't see the tops. At times, the way became so shaded it was hard to see, and she was forced to watch Ivar's back and hope she didn't trip. Ivar walked ahead of them, and Rafe was doing his best to stay next to her on the path, only dropping behind when the way through the forest became too narrow. She felt him behind her, and it made her uncomfortable. Though she had no proof, she felt as if he stared at her ass and the idea made her legs stiff.

In the forest, she caught glimpses of woodland creatures. Birds trilled in long blasts, the sound close enough to Earth to be recognizable and yet the tone was off. She caught blurs of bright blues and purples in the trees.

"I suppose planets develop close to the same way in order to support humanoid life," Jenna said, trying to make conversation while learning something about this newfound universe. "You have trees. We have trees. You have birds. We have birds. Though, they don't look quite the same."

"Our people lived on Earth long ago before human persecution forced us through the portals," Ivar said. "We were stronger, but humans were more in number, and we had no wish to kill so many over the actions of a few zealots. The Draig people were our allies, and so we came here together to live in peace. It is possible some of the creatures came through, and our ancestors would have brought seeds for planting."

"So you don't have wars? Everyone gets along?" Jenna asked. "What about the people who were here before you?"

"The planet was uninhabited," Rafe said.

"There are a few skirmishes. Not everyone agrees on the path we should take," Ivar answered.

"What do you mean they don't agree? What path?" Jenna felt Rafe beside her and glanced up at him.

"Not everyone believes that we should search for brides through the portal," Rafe said. "There are some who think it will taint the shifter bloodlines and bring doom upon us. It is a small faction, but very vocal. They tried to kidnap Princess Eve and force her back through the portal. Her husband stopped them."

"Brother, don't scare her. Such troubles are not for a woman's mind," Ivar scolded.

Jenna frowned. She knew Ivar was dominating in personality, but she didn't like that little show of sexism. "I can assure you I can handle politics."

"Of course you can," Rafe agreed. "The gods would only bless me with a strong woman."

"You really don't take no for an answer, do you?" Jenna did her best to look stern. She didn't feel threatened by Rafe, but couldn't decide if his persistence was charming or annoying.

"Not when your lips against mine said yes." He winked. "And your beautiful eyes gazing deeply into my—"

"What did you mean they kidnaped Princess Eve?" Jenna interrupted.

Ivar sighed loudly. "Just that. They took Princess Eve and tried to send her back through the portal. Prince Kyran—he is the Draig prince,

Finn's brother—went after her and brought her home."

"And that's it. They just want to expel the humans who come through? Nothing else?" Jenna took a deep breath and eyed the trees for danger. She didn't see anything threatening.

Rafe answered, "Oh, no, they wanted her dead. They just didn't want her body left where we could find—"

"Rafe, enough!" Ivar stopped walking and turned to face them. "There is no reason to alarm Lady Jenna. She is under my protection, and none will dare to harm her. That is the end of it."

"But they took the Draig princess," Jenna insisted, not wanting to stop such an important conversation because it made Ivar uncomfortable. "What is to stop them from taking me?"

"You might as well know. The Draig are good people and our friends, but by nature they are..." Rafe glanced at his brother.

"They are not Var," Ivar stated. "Dragon-shifters are very reserved by nature. They can fight, but they do not exude fierceness like the Var. They council and speak before facing a conflict, worrying about what every person in their kingdom might think. They are still trying to decide what to do about the faction who took Princess Eve. We cat-shifters are bolder by nature and do not debate our actions to the point of inaction. If someone took my wife," he paused and looked pointedly at Jenna," or my ward, I'd hunt them all down and make sure everyone knew never to try such a foolish endeavor again."

The speech was said with such confidence and surety that she had no doubt he would do just that. Jenna swallowed nervously at his continued stare. When he didn't look away, she nodded to signify she understood. Ivar nodded once and again led the way forward.

"So, Ivar," Jenna interrupted. "Or should I call you Lord Ivar since you all keep calling me m'lady?"

"You may call me either, Lady Jenna," Ivar said, easily leaping over a thick tree root growing across the path.

"I'm a little unclear about what being a ward entails." Jenna leaned over to brace her hands as she crawled over the root. Dusting them, she hurried to catch up to Ivar. The sound of Rafe's feet landed behind her.

"You are under my protection," Ivar said, again leaping over an obstruction in the path.

"Yes, I get that part. But what am I expected to do?" Jenna again had to climb over a tree root.

"Act honorably," Ivar stated as if such a thing should have been obvious. He leaped over two more roots.

Jenna stopped walking and put her hands on her hips as he kept going.

"May I assist you?" Rafe asked, touching her arm.

"Is he obtuse on purpose or just a..." Jenna bit her lip. She almost called Ivar an "ass" but thought better of it. He was her protector, after all.

"He is..." Rafe searched for the right word. "He is burdened."

"Burdened?"

"Yes. By duty, by family expectations..." Rafe offered his hand to help her step onto the root.

"And you are not burdened?"

"It is my duty to see to it my brother does not take life so seriously." Rafe stepped up and over before assisting her a second time.

"It is your duty to aggravate me," Ivar yelled back at them. He'd stopped and waited for them to finish climbing over the tree roots.

"How did he hear that?" Jenna whispered. "You weren't speaking very loudly."

"Shifters have extraordinary hearing compared to humans." Rafe's eyes flashed, changing color. A tiny shiver of pleasure worked its way through her, and

MICHELLE M. PILLOW

she tried to hide her attraction to him under the pretense of dusting her hands on her pant legs. "As well as vision."

"Stop harassing my ward," Ivar said.

Rafe chuckled. He glanced over her. "I am sorry I did not have a gown ready for you when you arrived. I promise you will have everything you need as soon as we arrive home."

"She is my ward," Ivar corrected. "I will see to what she needs."

Jenna held her arms self-consciously tight to her body. Did she look that much of a mess? Her shirt was wrinkled from having slept in her clothes. The walking had caused her to sweat a little, even though the temperature was moderate. She ran her fingers through her hair to comb it out. They hit a tangle, and she grimaced.

The path straightened, and they could again walk with ease. Rafe fell into step beside her.

"Does it hurt when you change into Var?" she asked, thinking of Rafe's shifting eyes.

"We do not change into Var," Ivar said. "We are Var."

"No, it does not hurt to shift," Rafe answered. "Being in cat form can often be more relaxing."

"How so?" Jenna asked.

"We are not expected to wear clothes." Rafe winked at her.

Jenna coughed in surprise at the bold statement.

"Rafe," Ivar scolded.

"Sorry," Rafe mumbled, before saying to Jenna, "We are not expected to wear clothes, *m'lady*."

Jenna couldn't help herself. She laughed. It didn't take much to deduce the family dynamics. The overly serious older brother was probably constantly scolding a mischievous younger brother who in turn became more rebellious. She probably shouldn't encourage Rafe's mischief, but she found herself saying, "So basically you're telling me there are a bunch of naked cats and dragons running around the planet?"

"No, m'lady," Ivar answered. "Draig remain clothed when they shift. As Var, we have the option of shifting partially into a man-cat—"

"Like I showed you outside the diner," Rafe inserted.

"—or completely into our animal form. As a man-cat, we can remain clothed. As a feline, we do not."

Rafe held up a finger. The tip extended into a pointed claw. He plucked lightly at the cross laces going down his chest. One pull and he'd cut out of his shirt almost instantly. "Would you like a demonstration?"

As much as Jenna did want to see such a thing, she looked at the commanding Ivar's back and said, "No, thank you."

They continued on. The forest became dense, and she dropped behind Rafe before he could let her go first. It was her turn to study him. There was an ease to which Rafe moved which could only be called a feline grace. His motions were smooth and confident. Ivar also had confidence, but his gait was more militant as if a heavy weight pressed down on him.

The path continued to narrow. Brush pressed along her left and marsh water spread out to the right. Her pace slowed, and she looked down to watch where she stepped. Seeing motion in front of her, she glanced up. Rafe had jumped off the ground and swung forward on a branch only to land with ease and keep going.

Jenna lost her footing and stumbled, slipping into the murky marsh water. The surface rippled. She started to laugh at her misstep when she noticed the water didn't stop rippling. Peeks of red streaked around her sunken foot.

"Snakes," Jenna whispered, trying to get Rafe's

attention. He'd moved up ahead. Her legs trembled. She slowly lifted her hand toward him. "Snakes."

Jenna had no way of knowing if the creatures were dangerous, but they swarmed her calf aggressively, brushing against her pant leg. She bit her lip to keep from crying out. Her eyes met Rafe's concerned ones. He turned his attention to the water.

"Don't move," he ordered. Rafe tapped his toes against the water several times. The swarm surfaced and darted away to hunt his foot. "Lift out."

Jenna obeyed as Rafe darted forward to steady her on the narrow path. Her heart beat hard. "I assume those are poisonous. Thank you."

Rafe brushed her hair from her face. His gaze held hers, and the familiar tingle of his nearness erupted all over her body. "I would battle a thousand givres for you, m'lady."

"Givre?"

His thumb moved along her bottom lip, and it was hard to concentrate past it. "You said snake? Yes, they are venomous."

Jenna looked at his mouth, remembering what it felt like when he kissed her. She wanted him to do it again. Her breathing deepened and she waited for him to dip forward.

"You protector is turning around to see why

we're taking so long." Rafe dropped his hand from her face but kept a steady hold on her arm. "Let me help you past. It won't be much longer now."

RAFE LOOKED for any excuse to touch Jenna, but it wasn't enough. He wanted her in his arms. He wanted to kiss her and touch her without the stares of his disapproving brother. None of this was as it should be. Jenna was meant to be his. Only the gods could have created such perfection for him. He wasn't looking for her, but he'd found her, and he wasn't going to let her go.

Jenna was his and in turn he was hers. For the rest of his days, he belonged to her. Three days ago he would have laughed at the very notion of such a feeling. Three days ago he'd been a complete and utter fool. He felt Jenna with every inch of his soul. How could Ivar not see it? How could Jenna not admit to their connection?

Rafe glanced to his side, wanting to again stroke his fingers along her magnificently red hair. Though he was confused by her reluctance, he was not disheartened. He would continue to offer himself to her, and she would one day accept. He just hoped that day was soon.

11

"*THIS IS YOUR HOME?*" Jenna stood at the gates of a castle that looked like it popped out of the Middle Ages and into reality.

They had come to a red wall constructed of earthen bricks in the forest and walked along the side until the stone opened to reveal a palace in a clearing. Trees surrounded the path that led around the outside wall. The red earthen wall matched the rectangular configuration of the castle. The corners had been built up into square towers, and narrow chimneys reached alongside them with gray smoke filtering from the tops. Bridges connected the tops of the towers, long open walkways that made her knees weak just looking up at them. If someone was to fall,

MICHELLE M. PILLOW

it would be at least a fourteen story drop to their death.

Lights radiated from the roof like a spotlight into the sky, dissipating into the expanse of green-blue overhead. It created a halo over the castle. Banners fluttered in the breeze along the length of the towers, held down so they didn't blow away. The Earth medieval-influenced design of a big gold cat stood boldly against the purple background. It made sense. They did say they used to live on Earth during that time.

Four sets of balconies circled around the main structure, one on each of the second to fifth stories. They were cut into the building rather than jutting out, shaded from the sunlight in sections with long strips of white gauze. She watched people walk past the openings in the material, none seeming to stop to look at them. A shout sounded as one man leaned over his balcony to look up. A woman waved down at him. Jenna's breath caught when the figure climbed onto the ledge and then leaped up to the next floor by way of the outside wall. The jump would have been impossible for a human man, but she was pretty sure she detected the guy to shift—though it was too far to see details.

"They are not supposed to go that way," Ivar stated in irritation.

"Seriously, you live here?" Jenna asked.

"Yes," Rafe said.

"But it's like a palace. Or are they apartments?" She squinted, seeing what could have been movement across the bridge walkway. It was too far for her to be sure.

"And I told you outside the diner, I am a prince." He motioned that she should walk through the front gate after Ivar. "Of course I would live in a palace."

"Yes, you did," she allowed, "but I have been focusing on the alien, cat-shifter, dragon-shifter part of that conversation."

Alien. Cat-shifter. Prince.

Jenna again hesitated and stopped walking.

"And when you accept me in marriage you will be a princess." Rafe smiled and stroked a piece of hair off her face.

Alien. Cat-shifter. Prince. Potential husband.

Out of all of those things, potential husband scared her the most. Though it was impossible, Jenna felt as if his fingers skimmed her nerves instead of strands of her hair. His eyes shifted color, and she couldn't look away. She shivered to feel his pull.

"So that must mean your parents are..." Jenna began, trying to keep her wits.

"King Ainmire and Queen Lassairfhina," Ivar stated. The stern tone effectively broke through her growing daze.

"Of course. King and queen." She swallowed nervously. Her mind whirled with thoughts. Rafe wanted to marry her. He wanted her to be a *princess*. She was to meet royalty. She was under the protection of royalty. So she'd be a curiosity to the people here. They'd be watching her, judging. Did they have tabloids here? Was she going to be in the spotlight? She didn't want to be in the tabloid spotlight. Well, as a human, they might be watching her anyway. And then there were those who didn't want her tainting their planet. Would she be safer at the palace with guards and stuff? Or would she be a bigger target to be made an example off. They did kidnap Princess Eve, so royalty didn't seem to stop them. And Rafe wanted to marry her and make her a princess. And...and...and...

Jenna took a step back toward the gate. Her breathing deepened and she tried not to hyperventilate. She slowly shook her head. "I shouldn't be here?"

"You're right. You should be inside." Rafe placed

his fingers on her elbow to urge her forward. Her thoughts were too scattered to protest. Each time she tried to hesitate, he would nudge her to walking.

The path leading up to the palace doors was flanked by floral ground cover. The tiny dots of white, gold and red colors spread over the yard. She took slow steps, trying to breath, trying to slow her pounding heart, still not sure she wanted to go inside while knowing she didn't have anywhere else to go.

The lights on top of the castle became brighter. Jenna stopped moving and looked up.

"Who arrives?" Rafe asked, not prodding her forward like before.

"It looks as if Roswell is delivering the new equipment I have negotiated for," Ivar answered.

A flying saucer dropped down from the sky. It didn't make any noise as it slowly descended on the rooftop, which was apparently a landing pad. It passed through the bridges and towers. Wind stirred, rushing against her body. Rafe placed his hand on back in a supportive gesture to keep her from stumbling.

When the wind died down, Ivar continued, "They are giving us something called a medical bed. It is able to attend wounds and help human frailties. We are also getting a hand-held device."

"What did you trade for it?" Rafe asked.

"Research. Anyone who wishes to use the bed must agree to have their treatments and outcomes reported back to the Reticulans so they may make advancements. It will also report any unknown illnesses for them to study. They were very enthusiastic over the prospect. I also told them about the planet's reproductive issues. They said they'd look into it as they gather more genetic research information from us."

"Why do they do it?" Jenna touched her head where the little gray men had fixed her concussion. "What is in it for them?"

"It is their religion to help as many people as they can. They started the Medical Alliance for Planetary Health to carry out that mission. Many aliens have benefited from their research." Ivar made his way toward the front entrance at a faster pace as the saucer landed out of sight.

"They have medical technology that can save lives, and my people kept asking to be anal probed," Jenna mumbled dryly. "Way to go, Earthlings. That would be an epic planetary fail."

They neared the castle entrance. The door had been left wide open, and no one stood guard. Ivar paused at the entrance and placed his hand against a stone. A woman appeared and reached to the side. The ornate pattern of her tunic dress hugged her many curves. The dark brown material matched her eyes. Blonde hair was pulled up to form a braided crown. When the woman touched the wall, the entryway tinted with transparent blue.

"What is that?" Jenna whispered to Rafe.

"It is called a guard shield. It lets the breeze pass, but it keeps intruders from walking inside without permission. The blue means it safe to cross." Rafe motioned her to go inside.

Jenna hesitated. "And clear means it's not safe? Then how do you know where it is and where you can walk if it's clear?"

Rafe tilted his head in question. "You did not see the activated shield?" Jenna shook her head in denial. "That would explain why Princess Eve walked into one. She couldn't see it with shifter eyes."

"Is it safe? Does it hurt to—" Jenna began.

Ivar took her wrist and pulled Jenna through the blue-tinted barrier before she could protest. She gasped in fright but didn't feel anything as she passed into the castle. "See. It is harmless."

"Ivar, you found a wife!" The woman released her hand from the stone and held out her arms in welcome. Her bright smile lit up her entire face.

"This is my ward," Ivar corrected. "Lady Jenna, my mother, Queen Lassairfhina."

"Ward?" The queen frowned and turned her full attention to Jenna.

"It's nice to meet you, Queen," Jenna hesitated briefly, "*La-sah-ree-nah.*"

The queen's expression fell. "I don't understand. Did you change your mind once you passed through the portal? What happened? Why do you not wish to marry Prince Ivar? My son is an honorable man. There is no reason you should deny him if that is what the gods want."

"I, uh..." Jenna looked helplessly at the two brothers. A man joined the queen and Jenna guessed he was King Ainmire by his bearing. That and the fact he brushed the backs of his fingers along the queen's arm. Age had apparently been very kind to the couple as they hardly looked old enough to be Rafe and Ivar's parents. King Ainmire could pass as Ivar's twin except for the shorter hair and scar running down the side of his neck.

"It was not my doing," Ivar stated. He nodded at Rafe. "Look to your other son for those answers."

"Rafe brought home a bride?" The king started to laugh, obviously thinking it was a joke. His accent was thicker than the rest of his family, but she understood him.

"If she is Rafe's wife, then why is she your ward?" The queen eyed both of her sons before settling on the youngest. "What did you do?"

"Rafe?" The king's laughter died when no one joined him. "What did you do?" Then, turning to eye Jenna with a combination of superiority and pity, he didn't give his son time to answer. "M'lady, did you follow Rafe through the portal? Did he seduce you and give you the wrong impression of his intentions? You would not be the first to fall for my wayward boy."

"I, ah..." Jenna stiffened. Was running away an option?

The queen arched a brow, clearly expecting her to answer.

"I didn't sleep with your son," Jenna blurted. She might look like a wreck with her tangled hair and dirty clothes, but she still had pride and these people basically accused her of having a one-night stand and not taking a hint the next morning. "I didn't ask to be brought here."

Instantly, both parents turned to Rafe with looks of dismay.

"What did you do?" the queen demanded.

"She likes cats and the gods—" Rafe began.

"Communication error," Ivar broke in. "Lady Jenna is under my protection until she decides to take a husband of her choosing."

"Which will be me," Rafe asserted. He smiled at Jenna. "If m'lady so decrees?"

"It's nice to meet you, King Ainmire," Jenna said weakly, not knowing what else to say. Did she bow? Curtsey? Lay prostrate on the ground? The idea to run away screaming still held a lot of appeal.

The king furrowed his brow. "Is she well? Did you drop her? She looks as if you tumbled her down the mountainside to get here."

"No, she ran into the pole on her own," Rafe answered.

"Roswell saw to that injury when we were with the dragons," Ivar added.

"Maybe have him look again," the king said. "The Reticulian ship is landing now."

"Lady Jenna, I apologize for my sons," the queen said. "Prince Rafe should not have brought you through the portal without an understanding. This reflects poorly on the Var—"

"Prince Finn helped me," Rafe defended. "Be mad at the dragons. They're the ones in charge of the portal."

"—and Prince Ivar should not have allowed it," the queen finished.

"Dragon-shifters," the king mumbled to himself. "Our ancestors should never have given them control over the portal. I do not like them regulating when my people can go through. Did you know the Draig king has now suggested we—"

"Your ancestors wanted to keep the Var people away from any human attack if they managed to find a way through." The queen tapped her husband's arm. "This is nothing to discuss in front of Lady Jenna."

The king answered her in the Var language. Jenna frowned, wondering what was being said. When they finished, the king said, "We should see why the Reticulans are back."

"I negotiated with them at the Draig encampment." Ivar joined his father. "If we are to have human mates we need to implement precautions for their fragility."

The men continued to converse, switching to the gruff Var language as they walked away.

"Lady Jenna, I will show you to your rooms. As Ivar's ward, you will take the guest chambers next to his." The queen turned, expecting her to follow.

"I can escort her," Rafe offered.

"No." The queen didn't look at him as she continued to walk. "You can join your father on the landing platform in welcoming our guests. I will speak privately with Lady Jenna."

RAFE WATCHED JENNA WALK AWAY. Her steps were stilted, and she glanced back at him several times. He lifted his hand and smiled at her reassuringly. She did not return the expression.

Frustration pounded through him. Why did everyone refuse to see what his soul knew?

As Jenna turned the corner, doubt began to fill him. What if he was wrong? What if she never accepted him as her husband? What if she took another?

Rafe didn't like feeling uncertain. Ignoring his mother's wishes that he go listen to polite conversation to which he had nothing to contribute, he slipped a claw under his laces and shifted fully into his panther form. The entryway had been left open, and he ran through the blue barrier back toward the forest, leaving his clothing behind him.

JENNA's new bedroom suite was a combination of a medieval palace, alien sci-fi, and homage to the crazy cat lady. Stone walls and floors, a tall wooden bed with canopied sides, narrow shuttered windows, and a fireplace were clearly medieval in design, as was the gray fur rug placed near the window.

Every surface seemed to be covered in cat statues, cat embroidery, cat paintings, cat tapestries, cat carvings...well, it was clearly a glimpse into her cat lady future had she not gone through the portal. And, apparently, it was her future having come through the portal as well. The only difference was on Qurilixen she was more pet to the cats versus their owner.

As the queen pointed out the hidden conveniences, the sci-fi part of her suite became most evident. Walls opened to reveal hidden nooks filled with toiletries, strange liquors, extra blankets, and others with grooming objects Jenna wouldn't be touching anytime soon. When the queen pressed a cat's statuesque head, a holographic screen projected before the fireplace. The flat image was of an old black-and-white movie. She vaguely recognized the dancing actors from Hollywood's Golden Age.

"Earth transmissions," the queen explained. "Our technicians capture them from space. It is how we learned to speak your language. When we first saw them, we didn't realize they'd come from our old home world until an elder recognized one of the old castles and the words."

The screen blipped mid-scene, and another show started. This one looked like an old Navy training film from the 1950s.

"These are Rafe's favorite," the queen said. "He had that same white tunic made for when he visits Earth."

Rafe liked dressing up like a sailor in bell bottoms? Jenna tried not to laugh at the imagery.

"Ivar is a draqueen," the queen added. "The scouts taught us that word. It is very royal and fitting for my oldest son."

Jenna snorted in an effort not to laugh. She covered her mouth and pretended to sneeze. "Excuse me. The forest was dusty."

The transmission blipped again, changing to an old cowboy flick.

"How did you change the channel?" Jenna asked to ease the subject away from the princes.

"Channel?"

"Channel. From one transmission to another? From the first movie to this one?" Jenna went to study the remote control cat.

"There is only this. They try to get complete transmissions when they can, but they are fragmented. However, the Draig have been trying to pull transmissions through the portals. They are supposed to send them to us, but I'm not sure...well, you don't need to hear about our political arrangements." The queen waved a dismissive hand. "Our database of transmissions is getting bigger. Although, we have had very little luck in getting them from visiting alien dignitaries though we have tried. There is not much call for Earth culture in the universes, so it's a specialized request."

Jenna reached for the screen, and her hand fell through the hologram. "Why don't you buy the movies you want when you travel to Earth? You appear to a have electricity. I'm sure something can be rigged." She paused, remembering she was talking to royalty. "I mean, it's just a suggestion, but that way you wouldn't have to wait for your neighbors to send you films."

"You can buy these at a marketplace?" The queen motioned to the holographic television and hummed softly. "The scouts did not report that to me."

"There are language videos, too. I think that would make it easier to learn from instead of watching movies. English is just one of the Earth languages though it's also one of the most widely known. Chinese might be useful. It's also widely used. Books might help as well. They'd give words to the language, not just sound, so your people could read and write as well as speak."

"The portal has brought the men to some locales were we have not been able to communicate. Normally we do not make trips during that time." Queen Lassairfhina nodded. "Thank you, Lady Jenna. This is very useful information. Perhaps there are reasons the gods had Rafe bring you to us."

"So the portal does not always go back to the same place?" Jenna touched the remote cat head. It turned beneath her finger, and a blast of sound hit her. She quickly turned the head back and pressed it, shutting the transmission off. She mumbled, "Sorry."

"The portal changes locations every night," the queen answered, "but it does follow a yearly cycle. Scientists say planet rotation. History says magic. Perhaps it is both. All I know is it saved the Var centuries ago and it saves them again now by giving the men a means to marry."

So she didn't have to wait a year to return home? Rafe and Ivar had both indicated otherwise.

"Tog-tog!" The queen exclaimed. Jenna jumped, startled. The woman crossed over to the gray fur rug. "There you are. I've been looking for you for days." She nudged it with her foot. The flat rug began to blow up like a balloon, taking the shape of a plump animal with six short legs. The queen stroked the creature's back.

"What is that?" Jenna asked. She couldn't make out a face in the furry blob.

"This is Tog-tog. He followed me to this planet. He shouldn't have, but I didn't have the heart to send him away, so I hid him in my chambers until my parents left. He roams the palace and is lost more often than not. He has apparently taken a liking to this room."

To prove her point, Tog-tog waddled away on his

short legs and then deflated in a new location on the other side of the bed.

"Try not to step on him," the queen said.

Jenna nodded in understanding, not sure what to make of the creature. "You were not born here?"

"No. I am Feenik by birth, Var by marriage. I met the king when my family landed here. They left, and I stayed." She gave a small smile as if remembering something Jenna could not know. "It was a long time ago and a story for another time. You look exhausted."

"I am. It's been a long couple of days."

"If you would like to bathe..." The queen moved across the room to a tiered platform in the corner and pressed a cat paw. The open space transformed. Stone parted to make a drain. Metal slid over the floors and down the walls. Tiny spouts came from between the ceiling stones and began to rain down. There was no curtain for privacy, but the design kept the water from flooding the rest of the room.

"Yes, thank you."

"Soaps. Drying linens. Hair cream." The queen brought the items to her attention. "My gowns will be too big for you, but I will see if I can find something suitable until Ivar can arrange for the dressmaker."

"Thank you."

"When you're ready for the servants to bring you a tray of food, press here." Queen Lassairfhina's hand brushed over an engraved button near the door. "Otherwise you should not be disturbed."

13

Jenna stood in the middle of the shower, letting the water rain down on her naked body. At first it had been a little too warm, but as her body adjusted she found she could barely move. Unlike home, there didn't seem to be an issue with running out of hot water.

What a strange life hers had become. She was taking a shower on an alien planet, the guest of royalty, surrounded by walking rugs and drag queen princes. She felt very sane, but if she wasn't she hoped the doctors didn't cure her too quickly.

And then there was Rafe. His kiss haunted her lips. If she allowed herself, to be honest, she liked it when he kissed her. She wanted him to do it again. And again. And again...

Her body ached and the hot shower didn't seem to cool her growing desires. Too bad he was so hell-bent on getting her to marry him. Otherwise, she might have been more inclined to explore where his kisses led.

But she was alone now. What harm could there be in letting her thoughts wander?

"Mm," she hummed thoughtfully as she remembered meeting him at the diner. He'd been so sexy and so presumably crazy. He had an open smile, playful, teasing, tempting. And his eyes... Damn, those eyes. She'd never seen eyes that penetrated so deeply. The man was walking temptation. When he looked at her, unconsciously licking his bottom lip, she felt him luring her in.

What would it be like to give in to him? Strong body against hers. That mouth on her breasts. Those hands skimming down her sides. His hips pressing open her legs. The tightness of his pants indicated his body was formed human enough to make it work.

The shower seemed to become hotter. She breathed deeply, and the water trailed over her lips. Her hands glided over her skin but did not seem to cure the ache building ever higher inside of her. Her nerves screamed for pleasure. Her sex needed to be...

A low growl interrupted her thoughts, and she gasped, turning to see what intruded into her room. She covered her privates the best she could and did not move out of the shower. A black jaguar stalked across the suite, his green eyes focused on her as if she were his prey.

She edged back, keeping her eyes on him and trying not to make any sudden movements. Jenna had no experience with wilderness survival and couldn't remember if she was supposed to be aggressive or submissive, run and scream or curl into a ball and play dead while hoping not to get mauled. And that was even if Earth rules applied here.

They're shifters, she reminded herself. "Who are you?"

The animal snorted by way of answer. She heard it over the falling water. It appeared the creature understood. His steps slowed.

"I think you have the wrong room. The queen said I could stay here."

The animal made a small throaty noise and came to the edge of the shower. He lifted his head as if sniffing for her.

"I'm under the prince's protection," she added weakly.

The animal crossed into the shower. The water hit his black fur. Jenna slowly backed toward the corner. It wasn't the best escape route. Fear trickled over her. Her heart pounded. This couldn't be it. She didn't journey to a new world just to be eaten by a wild animal. The princes had said there were those who didn't want humans on their planet.

The cat came before her. He bared his teeth.

"Please don't hurt me," she whispered.

Suddenly, the cat's head whipped around, and it ran for the opened door. Jenna slid to the shower floor. Her legs wouldn't hold her, and she crawled toward the edge of the falling water to get a towel.

She reached dry land and wrapped a thin towel around her body. As she hurried to close the door, it moved. She yelped as the cat came back. It rushed forward. She screamed and held up her hands. The towel dropped to the floor. The cat darted past her and ran around the room in a black blur of movement. It paused to examine Tog-tog before moving on. When it finished, it came to the wet trail of sloppy paw prints on the ground and then went to the door to shut it with his head, latching them in.

This time the green-gold eyes seemed gentler and the cat's movements less aggressive as it came for her. Jenna backed away. The shower hit her back, and she stopped. The cat looked her over, slowly. She gasped, again covering her privates.

"What do you want?" she demanded. "This isn't funny. You're...you're a *bad kitty!*"

As she watched, the animal began to shift. His body morphed and stretched. Jenna took a step out of the shower toward the fallen towel, careful not to get too close.

It didn't take long before Rafe's changing features became recognizable. Jenna pulled the towel to her chest. Angrily, she said, "I should have known it was you!"

When he'd fully turned into his human form, he stayed knelt before her—crouched and naked, eyes peering up at her to do wicked things to her senses.

"Bad kitty?" He sounded amused. The side of his lip curled.

"I was told I'd have privacy," Jenna said. It was hard to ignore the fact that they were both naked with only her thin towel providing coverage.

"I was told you like cats." He pushed up, muscles rippling with the gracefully purposeful movement. Rafe didn't bother to hide the evidence of his desire for her. It towered from his hips. His playful smile grew as he looked her over. "But do you like bad?"

Jenna shivered, trying not to let herself become aroused. "What do you think you're doing?"

He grinned as if the answer was obvious. She couldn't think with him standing all confident and naked in front of her. His erection kept her attention, the thick length of his shaft nothing to be ashamed of. There was nothing alien about the shape of him in this state.

"Cover your, your, your..." She gestured at his crotch, trying to think of the most unsexy way of saying it. "Manroot!"

"Manroot?"

"Your thingy."

"My...?"

"Your penis!" she cried. "Cover your penis."

Rafe arched a brow and reached for his cock. He placed his hand over it. "This?"

"Yes." She began to nod.

Rafe stroked the length. His voice lowered. "This?"

Jenna started to shake her head in denial.

Rafe came swiftly forward. He grabbed her by her hips and pressed her tight against him. "Or like this?" Rocking into her through the towel, he gave a small moan of pleasure. Then, with a hard pull, he yanked the thin towel from between them, so naked flesh hit naked flesh. "Or how about like this?

Jenna was too stunned to react. Rafe's hands roamed freely over her sides and back, holding her against him. He gripped her ass. It didn't take much to rekindle the desire she'd felt for him moments before.

"Don't deny what's between us," Rafe whispered. The tickle of his breath was warm against her ear. He maneuvered his body, so she was forced back into the shower. The water hit them, tiny caress that eased the way of his fingers. It trickled down her breasts, moistening her stomach so that he began to slide more easily when he rocked against her.

Jenna couldn't think of a reason not to let him touch her. Lips and tongue found her neck and ear. Before she realized it, she was exploring the length of him. His firm ass flexed against her hands.

Rafe grabbed her wrist and pulled her hand around to his cock. He held her fingers around him, using them to stroke. He kissed her, hard, moaning loudly into her mouth. Water lubricated their lips, their hands, his arousal. His grip on her hand tightened and he continued to run her fingers up and down.

"Kiss me here." His stroking hand paused to indicate his meaning. The request sounded almost like a demand. He released her hand from his shaft and gently pressed her hips downward to get her to kneel. "I need to be eased."

Jenna made a weak noise. This man was so confident, so sure she'd do what he said. Part of her thought to protest out of principal. It was overridden by the fact her knees were bending and her hands were steadying her journey to the shower floor.

Rafe pressed two fingers between her lips and teeth to make her mouth part wide. He then took his cock and angled it to her. Pulling her by the mouth, he slipped his arousal past her lips before removing his fingers to grab the back of her head. He swayed his hips back and forth to move the tip of his cock around in her mouth. His fingers worked against her hair.

"Kiss it," he begged. Jenna puckered her lips around him. He stopped swaying and began thrusting the tip in her mouth. At first it was shallow but the more excited he became, the deeper he tried to plunge. She lifted her hands to his thick shaft, partly to stroke him, partly to keep him from choking her.

Both hands found her head. She sucked harder.

He jerked, finding release into her mouth. Rafe let go of her head and joined her on the shower floor. Kneeling, he cupped her face and leaned in to kiss her.

A loud knock sounded, and Rafe pulled way before their lips could meet. His eyes flashed as he looked toward the door. He stood, helping her to her feet. "Are you expecting someone?"

"Who would I be expecting?" Jenna asked. "Though the queen did say something about a dressmaker.

The knock sounded again, louder and faster.

"It's my brother," Rafe stated.

"How do you know?"

"I'd know his irritation anywhere." Rafe gave a small laugh and moved as if to answer the door naked.

"Hide." Jenna grabbed his arm and stopped him.

"Excuse me?"

"Hide." She pulled him toward the bed. "Get under the bed."

Rafe grinned in amusement as he went to obey.

"One moment please," Jenna yelled. She looked at her dirty Earth clothes on the floor and kicked them aside. Hurrying to the bed, she pulled off the top covers and wrapped them around her body.

Rafe's hand came out from underneath to caress her ankle. She lightly kicked him off. His laugh sounded, and she leaned over to whisper. "Be quiet."

"As m'lady so decrees," he whispered back.

Jenna wrapped the covers around her like a dress. She pushed her wet, messy hair behind her shoulders and went to the door. Rafe was right. It was her guardian.

"Hi, sorry, I was not sure how to shut off the shower." Jenna tried to act innocent.

Ivar held a stack of clothing. He stepped into the room and placed them on a wooden chair. "I was told you need the services of a dressmaker. Until it can be arranged, I brought you these." Next he moved to the shower cat and pulled its paw. The water stopped raining, and the shower began the retraction process. "Do you require anything else, m'lady?"

"No, thank you," Jenna said. She purposefully did not look toward the bed and kept her eyes on Ivar.

"There is a feast tonight in honor of your coming." He lifted is hand to gesture to the button the queen showed her. "Press here if you need assistance."

"I will. Thank you." Jenna forced a smile and waited for him to leave.

"Rafe, make sure she makes it to the feast on time," Ivar commanded.

Jenna held her breath.

"Yes, brother," Rafe answered just as loudly.

Jenna closed her eyes and didn't move.

"If he bothers you, scream and I will come," Ivar said. She heard the door close behind him.

Jenna remained with her eyes closed.

"Lady Jenna?" Rafe called playfully. "How long would you like me to remain in hiding?"

"You suck at being discreet," she mumbled. Then louder, she added, "I thought I told you to be quiet."

"It's dusty down here," he complained.

"That's your punishment for scaring me." Jenna went to examine her new wardrobe. The gown looked like a simpler version of the queen's—bodice with laces, long skirt, capped sleeves. The second dress was more of a white frock. Opting for the more comfortable version, she pulled it over her head.

"What if I apologized? I came in from a run and thought I heard you in danger, but I was mistaken. Then I saw you and... What are you doing?"

"You were the danger. I thought you were going to eat me." She smoothed down the gown and crossed to where the toiletry items were hidden in the wall cupboard.

Rafe slid his head and shoulders out from under the bed. He grinned. "I was going to eat you but we were interrupted."

"You know what I mean." Jenna grabbed a handle-less brush and set to work on her hair, anything to keep her hands busy. "I'm talking about the first time you came in here."

"The first time?" His grin held a few moments before falling. He pushed out from under the bed and moved toward her. When she didn't stop brushing, Rafe took her wrist and forced him to look at her. "What do you mean the first time?"

"The first time," she stated. She forced her wrist from his hold and finished brushing her hair. She pulled a little too hard and fast while trying not to look at the fact he was still delectably naked. "When you came in here, cornered me in the shower and then ran out only to come back in seconds later and stalk around the room."

Rafe looked around the room as if something might materialize. "Jenna, that wasn't me. Why would you think I came in here?"

"You transform into a black jaguar."

"I'm what you call a black panther."

"Black panther is a catch-all term for several types of cats with black fur. In America—"

"You're saying you thought you saw me twice?" Rafe stiffened. "I'm not the only one with black fur. It's a common trait amongst the Var."

"That wasn't you?" Jenna dropped the brush. "You're serious. That wasn't you. Then who was it? Why did they want to hurt me?"

"I don't know. Maybe he smelled your, ah, scent like I did and couldn't resist coming in?"

"No. If it wasn't you playing around, then I'm pretty sure that cat wanted me dead. I don't know why it stopped unless he heard you coming." Jenna's heart started to pound, and she felt lightheaded.

"No one will harm you." Rafe sounded so sure of that fact. "I will find who threatened you and they will have to answer for it. Until then palace guards will be placed in the hall outside your chambers, and I will not leave your side."

"You plan on staying in this room with me?"

"Or we can move to my chambers." He touched her damp hair. "You are my bride."

Jenna shook her head in denial.

"You are very contrary," he said in frustration. "I know you feel us."

"And you are a hardheaded pain in the ass. All you think about is getting married. Have you actually thought about what it would be like to actually *be* married?"

Rafe looked at the bed and grinned.

Jenna hit him on the chest. "Relationships are complicated and take work. We don't know each other. What job will I have? Will we want children? If we have children how will we raise them? Do we have the same values? How will we live? How—"

Rafe placed his fingers over her mouth and slowly shook his head. "You think too much. Your job will be as a princess. Of course, we will have children. We will raise them as our children. I value you, and we will live as husband and wife. These are not complicated questions."

He seemed so sure. Jenna didn't know if she wanted to hit him or kiss him. She pressed her palms to her closed eyes. "You are so frustrating."

"And you are stubborn."

Jenna dropped her hands. "I'm hungry. When is this feast happening?"

"Put the rest of your dress on and I'll take you." He pointed in one direction. "Ivar is that way." He pointed the other direction. "My chambers are just down the hall. I'm going to dress and come back for you. If you scream, I'll hear it. If you whisper, I'll hear it. No one will hurt you. I swear my life on it."

"Thank you," Jenna said as he opened the door to go.

"You are welcome, m'lady." He shut it firmly behind him.

"But you're still a pain in the ass," she mumbled.

Rafe's laughter sounded outside the door before fading as he moved down the hall.

14

"It cannot be a coincidence that someone threatens Lady Jenna the first moment she is alone." King Ainmire studied his sons. The sound of the dining hall filtered through his office door, and he moved to shut the noise out. A low fire burned, casting orange light over black shadows. Ivar sat before the fire, an ankle resting on his knee. He seemed more interested in the fire than the conversation, but Rafe knew his brother considered everything.

Rafe had left Jenna with his mother, overlooking the gathered crowd. Nothing would happen to her in such a public place. Even so, he wanted to go back to her side.

"And you're sure no one followed you in the

forest?" The king leaned against the mantel to face his sons.

"No one," Ivar stated.

Rafe stood behind a chair, resting his arms on the back. He dropped his eyes to the empty seat cushion. "My thoughts were occupied elsewhere, but I did not detect a threat."

"I knew the Nutef faction was becoming more vocal but I did not imagine they would dare to try anything in our home. This goes too far. It is one thing to kidnap a Draig princess, but another to threaten a royal Var ward." The king's face shifted partially into his tiger form in his anger. "Why can't they see we opened the portal to help the people? Our ancestors mated with humans. They are the perfect vessels to carry our children."

"They claim it was the human-shifter mating that drove us from the Earth," Rafe said.

"Rewriting history to fit your doctrine does not make it true," the king interjected.

"They gain more support," Ivar said. "They are no longer content to preach against cat-dragon marriage. The old stories still linger in the villages. People fear the human world. We have seen this world, father. It is chaotic. Culturally, humans are still children. Maybe it is their shorter life spans.

They have little time before the next generation takes over."

"Our people fear them only because they don't understand them," Rafe said. "The humans are not children. They are just different than we are. It does not make them better or worse."

"Have you seen them in their revelry? Puking on their streets? Drunken fools fighting and preening?" Ivar gave a short, humorless laugh. "They have plenty women but the good ones are rare. We have been where the unmarried gather to find mates. Sadly, I think those women even understand they can never be royalty. I tell them I am a draqueen, and they instantly go in search of other mates. It is a wonder they manage to perpetuate a culture at all. Their process is barbaric. They even finger shackle each other because their bonds are not strong enough to radiate for all to see."

"Fear is born of ignorance," the king stated. "But we will not change Nutef opinions with a couple of marriages. It will take time to prove there is nothing to fear from human wives. If the human armies try to march through the portal—if they can even find the way in—then we kill them as they come through, one by one. If by some fluke they make it across, then they will have to fight through dragon territory before reaching us. Our people have nothing to fear."

"The sooner more women are brought through, the better it will become." Rafe thought of the way he felt when he was with Jenna. Nothing about that could be evil or wrong. "They'll see their fears are unfounded. They'll see the happiness of mated couples."

"Happiness in mating? What did those humans do to my son?" the king teased. Rafe ignored him.

"That plan might prove challenging," Ivar said, sharing a look with his father.

"Why?" Rafe straightened and crossed his arms over his chest.

"The Draig have proposed we only go through the portal on the night of darkness." They wish to make it a sacred celebration and the only time men can find mates." King Ainmire's eyes flashed and remained shifted.

"But that is only once a year," Rafe said. With three suns, their planet was always cast in light except for the one night of darkness a year. "Why would we limit our search to one night?"

"Control over the portals," Ivar said. "To keep people from sneaking through like the one who kidnaped Princess Eve."

"Refuse the proposal." Rafe crossed over to the door and pulled it open a crack to listen to the hall before shutting it again. Jenna was safe. "Think of how many trips it took me to find Lady Jenna, how many places we traveled. If we only go once a year..."

"The odds are not in our favor," Ivar finished.

"I fear we might not have much of a choice. These things have to be handled carefully. Being far away from the portal gave our people safety from any potential human invasions, but it also gave the dragon's control over it. We can't risk them locking us out or trapping us on the other side." The king leaned his head back and pressed his fingers to the bridge of his nose. "The Draig are our allies. We have no reason to doubt their intentions, but I have the Var future to think about. I will let them know I do not like the idea of limiting portal travel to one night. The need is too great."

"It's a bad idea for both peoples—cat and dragon," Rafe said. "One by one is hard enough. We need more women."

"I am not sure what to think of your sudden passion on the matter," the king said, "but if this is Lady Jenna's influence than I welcome it. You have bowed out of Var politics for too long."

"We can't very well grab a bunch of females and

let them loose in hopes that they find a mate," Ivar said. "But I also don't like the idea of my future being in the hands of the dragons' fears. I don't want to see the portals closed or limited, but should that happen we need an alternate plan. I say we more actively pursue offworld relations."

"The Draig do not want more aliens coming here," Rafe said. He would naturally do his duty by his family, but the dragons were his friends. He had grown up running the forests with Prince Finn. "They make valid points, too. We have lived centuries in peace because we kept to ourselves."

"We won't make an issue out of it, at least for now." The king straightened. "But I agree, we will continue to encourage interplanetary relations. I met the queen in such a way. If we are lucky, the Nutef faction will die out because they refuse to take non-shifter wives."

Ivar chuckled.

"Until then, they are a threat," Rafe insisted.

"Lady Jenna will be protected," the king assured him. "And we will find the man responsible for threatening her."

15

JENNA'S SMILE was frozen on her face. She knew she must look like a crazy person, knew her eyes were too wide and her gestures too measured. How could they not be? She was eating on a freaking stage like a sideshow curiosity. The only thing missing from her personal zoo exhibit was steel bars, manmade rock landscape, and a sign that read, "Jenna Kearney, Homo sapiens, Earth. Please do not feed the animals. They are on special diets."

She tried to focus on anything but the numerous eyes staring at her. Like the rest of the palace, white gauze strung over the red stone walls. Arched windows let light into the room, revealing the long stretch of landscape below. They were on the fifth story overlooking the front yard and forest. A low blue sun rested above the tree line, which made staring in that direction hard.

Tables were set around the hall, below the stage she was on. The queen roamed the floor, making the rounds to talk to her subjects. The low murmur of voices surrounded her but did not engage her. Jenna eyed the door where Rafe disappeared with his brother and father. The only ones who approached were servants who placed small trays of food in front of her. She ate because she was starving after a breakfast of berries in the forest. There were various meats and fruits, a blue-tinted bread, and a pasty substance that smelled like uncoated vitamins and tasted like what she imagined to be moist cattle feed.

When the food was cleared, and she was still left sitting alone, Jenna tried to keep smiling. After many long, uncomfortable minutes, she finally decided to excuse herself. She stood slowly, intent on making her way to the door. The second she was on her feet, ready to step down, the gathered crowd stopped talking amongst themselves and turned their full attention to her.

Jenna froze. They all watched her, expectantly. The queen straightened from where she leaned over a table and tilted her head.

"Ah, thank you for a lovely meal," Jenna said, her

words quiet. She cleared her throat. "You have a lovely, ah, palace."

They continued to stare.

"I like..." Jenna glanced around, not finding anything to help her with her unprepared speech. "Liked the bread. It was good. Excuse me."

She awkwardly bowed her head and walked quickly to the door. Once she was out of the dining hall, she jogged to the enclosed stairwell and made her way to the fourth floor to find her guest suite. Shutting herself inside, she leaned against the door and took a deep breath.

Tog-tog was draped over the back of the couch, it's fur not moving. Apparently, the rug monster liked being her roommate.

"I liked the bread it was good?" She smacked her palm against her head.

"Lady Jenna?" She heard her name before a loud knock sounded at the door. "M'lady?"

Jenna suppressed a groan and moved to pull open a door. The man wore a Var shirt with an embroidered cat emblem on the chest. Rafe had told her it was the symbol of the palace guard. "Yes?"

"I am Hector, m'lady. Prince Rafe ordered me to stand guard until the threat has passed. Are you in any danger within your chambers?" The guard had the kind of militant expression that said he took his job very seriously. Considering what his job entailed that was most likely a good thing.

Jenna needlessly looked over her shoulder and then back at him. She shook her head in denial. "No. I don't think so."

"May I enter on the prince's command?" Hector insisted.

Jenna vaguely wondered what he'd do if she refused. Instead, she opened the door wider and let him inside. As Hector searched the suite, she stayed by the open door. Another guard waited in the hall. She gave him a tight smile, and he bowed in her direction, "m'lady," before stiffly resuming his post. Neither man appeared threatening or aggressive, but she watched them carefully. The silence felt awkward, but she didn't know what to say to start a conversation with the men.

Catch my dinner speech? Yeah, I should be in politics.

Did you happen to catch the transmission of the sailor mopping the deck? Good stuff, right?

So, do you like being a cat-shifter? Have any hopes or dreams? I'd like to interview you for the school paper.

Cough up any good fur balls lately?

Jenna pretended to cough to hide her laugh.

I hope you guys can't secretly read minds.

Heavy footsteps sounded in the stairwell down the hall. She stepped back into the room ready to close herself in with Hector if there was danger. Rafe appeared, running full speed toward them. As he slid to a stop in front of her, Hector said behind her, "It is safe, m'lady."

"Ah, thank yo—" Jenna tried to answer, but Rafe took her by the arm and pulled her into the suite. Hector stepped out as Rafe moved in. He slammed the door behind him. "Rafe, what—?"

Rafe cupped her face and kissed her. His mouth pressed almost desperately along hers. His hands slid down her neck, pausing at her throat as if to test her pulse before moving lower to feel her chest and arms. The brush of fingers to her nipples jolted awareness down to her stomach. Her lungs began to burn for air, and she pulled her head back.

"What are you doing?" she demanded.

Rafe continued his examination of her body, going so far as to kneel to touch her legs. "You're not injured. I don't smell blood. Do you need the medical bed? It is ready for use."

"Injured?" Jenna grabbed his wrists as he made the journey back up her body. She squeezed tightly to get his attention. "What are you talking about? I'm fine. What is going on out there?"

"They told me..." Rafe lifted his hands, his strength not hampered by her hold on him. He again cupped her face and studied her eyes. "You ran from the hall."

"I didn't run," she protested in embarrassment. Perhaps she didn't walk out of the dining hall with as much dignity as she'd first thought. "I just..."

"It is all right. No one expects you to face the Nutef. You did the right thing in coming in here where your guards can keep you safe. We all know humans are fragile and—"

"What the hell is a *Nutef*?" Jenna asked in alarm. She jerked her head out of his grasp.

"The shifter threat against you. It has to be the Nutef faction. They are the most vocal about not wanting human mates brought to the planet. They believe with enough time and faith the gods will send us more cat-shifter females to marry. They are idealists."

"And they're here? Now?" Jenna looked at the door and took an unconscious step back. "And you sent Hector to check my room for them?"

"Did you not see them? You ran from—"

"I didn't run," Jenna insisted. "I was done eating

and I left. Everyone was staring at me, and I felt like a freaking zoo animal on display."

"So you did not see...?"

"You left me alone up there," Jenna accused. "The queen just dropped me off, told me to enjoy and spent the entire meal walking around talking to people. What was I supposed to do? Be a good little monkey and sit on display smiling until everyone was finished eating?"

"You were in the position of honor, so all may know who you are and how important you are to this family." Rafe made a move to reach for her again, but she stepped back. "Any one of them would have been happy to approach you if you so wished it. Even the queen did not eat with you out of respect. The king, Ivar and I left the hall so that you may have all the attention."

"No one told me that," Jenna stated. "And, for the record, I didn't want all the attention."

"I thought your place of honor would have been obvious. Of course the people would want to be introduced to you," Rafe said. "You are Lady Jenna."

Jenna didn't know what to say.

"Now that your honor in this household has been established, you will not have to be a good little monkey again. Next time I will sit with you."

Jenna couldn't help it. She tried to suppress her laugh but couldn't. Rafe was so earnest when he referred to her as a monkey. These people were obviously smart and could pick up language cues, but they didn't always get them right.

"I like when you smile," he said.

"How badly did I mess up the dinner?"

"It is fine that you did not speak to anyone," Rafe said as if thinking to himself. "They will think you're dignified, and all know you face a threat."

"I spoke to the servants," Jenna said, feeling somewhat defensive. She wasn't completely rude. "I thanked them."

"Dignified and benevolent," Rafe amended. "The servants would have brought you a wide variety of food to try so that they may learn your preferences. The fact you thanked them for it will show you have a kind heart. You did very well, m'lady."

They got all of that out of her being polite to the wait staff?

"Oh, no." Jenna bit her lip. She thought of the moist cattle feed she'd forced herself to eat and couldn't imagine what it would be like to have to partake of it daily. "I didn't know what they were doing. What if what I ate was not my preferences?"

"Why would you eat something you did not like?"

"I was trying to be polite and eat a little of everything. I didn't want to insult anyone." Jenna wrinkled her nose. "Please tell me there is a way to undo my choices."

"Of course. You just have to tell them."

"So what happens now? Is everyone panicked because they think the Nutef are out there?" Jenna rubbed her temples. "I feel like I messed everything up. I wish someone would have explained to me what to expect. Now it sounds like the entire guard is out there looking for something I didn't see. And you said it yourself, the cat who came in here is probably gone by now having failed, or maybe his mission was to simply scare me in which case it worked."

"The people will think you are brave to sit openly while there is a Nutef threat," Rafe said. "We were searching the palace already, so there is nothing for you to worry about."

"That is if there is even a threat. Maybe it was just some kid playing a prank or someone curious to see the human." Jenna didn't like all the attention the people of the palace were giving her. She didn't want spotlight treatment—people monitoring what she liked to eat, needing the royal guard to protect her, observing what kind of person she was.

"I promised to protect you and I will." This time when he reached for her face his touch was gentle. His eyes captured hers. "Nothing is going to happen to you, Jenna."

"Nothing?" Jenna looked at his mouth. Each time he touched her it became harder to resist. "I'm not sure I believe you."

"I will protect you," he said. "I will make you a fine husband."

"What if I don't want a fine husband?" Jenna wanted to kiss him. If she were honest with herself, she wanted to do a lot more than that.

"You want an inferior husband?"

"What if I don't want a husband at all right now," Jenna said. "We just met, Rafe. Does it have to be all or nothing?"

"Why would I not offer all?" He was so earnest.

"What I'm saying is you don't have to." How was it she was the one trying to convince the sexy man to keep it casual? "Can't we just have fun and not worry about marriage and children and mortgages—if you even have mortgages?"

"Mortgages?"

"Borrow money to pay for a house," she explained.

"People build their houses," Rafe answered. "So no, we do not have to worry about that."

"You're straying off point."

"Are you concerned we would not have a home? There is no need. We will live here in my parents' home. Yes, we may have fun and of course we will have children when we marry, if the gods so bless us. The children will live here as well."

Jenna sighed, realizing she had to be blunter. "Rafe, try to hear me."

"I can hear you. I am standing right here." He motioned down to his feet.

"I don't want to get married right now. I do want to kiss you again. If that kissing leads to more, then I don't want to get pregnant right now. I have a doctor that gives me hormone shots to keep that from happening. I've been on them since college."

"You wish to be lovers." It was more of a statement than a question. Rafe seemed to ponder her words before nodding. "Yes, I will gladly lead to more." He tugged his laces and pulled the shirt over his head.

Jenna watched him move with predatory grace as he led her to the couch. He urged her to take a seat.

At first, she wasn't sure what he was up to, but then he began stripping out of his clothes. She leaned back to enjoy the show when her head bumped against the rug monster. She turned to see Tog-tog inflating. The creature rolled from the back of the couch onto the floor.

Rafe's hand on her leg brought her around to face him. He knelt naked before her, pulling her shoes off her feet. Green eyes peered into hers as his warm hands moved up her legs. Her breathing deepened as she waited to see what he would do. She remembered his taste from the shower, the intimate slide of moisture between them.

His fingers reached her thighs. A playful grin curled the side of his mouth as he lifted his arms. Her skirt fluttered up, and he disappeared under. When the material settled over his head, he pulled her forward.

Jenna automatically grabbed hold of the couch. Her hips met the edge of the seat. Rafe drew his mouth to her sex. When she tensed, he placed a leg over his shoulder. He gripped her hips to hold her in place. The ache that had stirred since meeting him flooded to the surface. She watched the shape of his head move under the skirt, aggressively dipping to match the licking of his tongue. Whenever she jerked or moaned, he would repeat the gestures relentlessly until he'd found her perfect rhythm.

Jenna gripped the cushion behind her head as she shook in violent release. Rafe emerged from beneath her dress with supernatural green eyes flashing in pleasure. His expression revealed pride in what he'd done.

She breathed heavily and could barely move. Rafe took advantage of her state and lifted her from the couch. He carried her swiftly across the suite to the bed. A single claw grew from his fingertip, and he cut the ties of her gown so that he could disrobe her—first the tunic dress and then the underdress. His arousal caught her notice, and she reached for his shaft. He fumbled in his efforts. When he had her naked and stirring, he crawled over her and braced his weight.

"I will examine my lover." Rafe cupped her pussy and slid a finger inside. "You feel pleasurable."

At first, Rafe made love to her slowly, savoring her body with his hand and mouth. He kissed her lips, her breasts, her stomach. He explored every inch of flesh he could reach, stroking her from her toes up to her hair. The red strands against her skin seemed to fascinate him as he drew the locks across her chest. His eyes gazed deeply into hers.

Jenna found herself following the ridges of his chest muscles, tracing them. She moaned softly whenever he found a particularly sensitive part of her body. The intense pleasure became too much. She hooked her legs behind him and tried to pull his hips into her.

Rafe reached between them, aiming himself. That first brush of thick contact caused her to inhale sharply and tense. Graceful hips pressed forward, the stroke of him like a dance between their bodies, tiny undulations that brought his shaft deeper. Jenna tried to follow his lead, but the tiny ripples of pleasure she felt made it hard to move.

Rafe braced his weight on his hands. The strokes became longer and smooth. The primal thrust of his body showed in each of his working muscles. His eyes remained shifted and focused on the bounce of her breasts. He thrust harder, seeming to take pleasure in the way it forced her chest to move. The movement of his hips forced her legs to fall from behind his back onto the bed.

Rafe put every part of him into pleasing her. His feet pressed into the bed. His legs tensed. His hips pumped. His chest heaved. His lips parted to let loose a low, animalistic sound of dominance. His hands gripped the bed on either side of her. She'd never been fucked with such intensity and passion.

Jenna came, knowing she had been fully conquered. Climax vibrated through her entire being. She was only vaguely aware of Rafe's pleasured release joining hers. Every nerve tingled. Each muscle tensed. Then came the drained aftermath when her body refused to move any more.

She'd been attracted to him from that first moment, but she could not have known just how fierce of a lover he would turn out to be. Such pleasure had never been known to her. If Rafe came to her again, there would be no resisting.

16

"WHAT ABOUT DATING?" Jenna relaxed into Rafe's hold. He cuddled her from behind, refusing to leave her room for her "protection". Time drifted, and she was sure she'd dozed, but she had no way of knowing for how long or how deep. His hands possessively roamed her naked body, and she wondered if he hoped to initiate another round.

"Dating?" Rafe's fingers threaded through her hair. He seemed obsessed with touching it.

"Yes," Jenna nodded. "What if we tried dating exclusively? We like each other so why not go slowly and see where this leads."

"Explain those terms."

"We don't have sex with other people," she said.

"We do things together. You do nice things for me. I do nice things for you. We talk. We—"

"That sounds like mating," he interrupted.

"Close, but we're not married," Jenna told him. "If it doesn't work out we can part ways. Like a practice run."

"You will succumb to me yet," he assured her, kissing the back of her neck. "Already you have agreed to be my lover. And I do not think you need more practice at it."

"Do you mate with everyone you have sex with?" Jenna asked, wondering if she'd misunderstood part of the custom along the way. There was so much to learn, and slight confusion over word translations did arise at times.

"Of course not. Why would I want that many wives?"

That many? I'm not sure I needed to know all that, Rafe. Jenna grimaced and mumbled aloud, "There is such a thing as oversharing."

"I do not mind. I like sharing stories with you." Rafe pulled her closer and became fascinated with kissing and stroking the back of her neck. "There are tales of those who have taken several half-mates but it is an old practice, one we mostly left behind on Earth when Var women were plentiful, and many Var men had died in battle or had been murdered by the human zealots."

"Var women could not take human husbands instead?"

"Some did," Rafe allowed, "but when they were discovered by the zealots the results were most horrific for the human mate. They were very dark times. For some reason, children born to a human man and cat-shifter woman did not always shift as they should." He ran his hand over her hip suggestively. "The pairing works much better when it is a Var man and a human woman. Wouldn't you agree?"

"I was serious about not wanting to get pregnant." Jenna felt him stiffen and pull away from her nape.

His tone was soft, and she could hear the hurt pouring out of him even as he tried to hide it. "I know my family thinks me irresponsible and rebellious, but I assure you I will make a good father. Is this why you do not wish to marry me? You do not think me capable of being a good mate?"

"Rafe, I—"

He sat up, cutting her off. "I assure you, I do my duty."

She turned to study his naked back.

"My parents rule this kingdom. They make the

decisions. Ivar is the future king, so his word carries weight in political matters. By the time they get around to asking me the decisions have already been made, and it's more of a courtesy. Traditionally as the younger son my role would have been to lead armies to battle so that the future king was not risked. As it stands, we are not at war, and I merely have to command the palace guard. They have been doing their jobs for centuries, so there is no reason for me to follow them around barking orders. Every few years I call the men to practice their battle skills, and the younger boys learn what they need to from their fathers and teachers."

Knowing she'd touched a raw nerve, she placed her hand on his back. "I do not question that you can do your job."

"It is my duty," he stated.

"I do not question that you can do your duty," she amended.

"And yet you do not think me good enough to father your children." He shook off her hand and moved to stand.

Though he appeared completely comfortable walking naked in front of her, Jenna was a little more modest and pulled the covers to hide her nakedness. It was one thing when he was looking at her in passion and quite another when he paced in frustration.

"Rafe, why does it have to be all or nothing with you?" Jenna hugged the blankets tighter. "Why not take it slow and see where this leads?"

"Because I feel it." He hit his hand against his chest. "I want it."

"Well, I feel confused," Jenna answered, her tone rising to match his. "I'm not like you. I'm not a cat-shifter. I don't know anything about this world, not really. It's all new and confusing, and the last thing I want is to throw marriage and children into the mix. That's not fair to either of us, and it's not fair to any child we'd bring into this world. What if we don't work out? What if you decide I'm too moody in the mornings? Or we run out of things to say? What if your habits drive me crazy? What if we get bored with each other's company after the newness of sexual attraction wears off? Marriage is a lot more than a feeling. It's a commitment."

"I know that," he answered loudly.

"Do you?" Jenna pushed to her knees. "We can't even talk about this without you getting upset and yelling at me. How are we actually going to be married if we can't even have this conversation?"

"You are yelling at me," Rafe answered, swinging his hands to his sides.

"And another thing, I don't even know what my options are here. I didn't like being put on display for everyone to stare at. I can't imagine being a princess and having my every move watched. I like being invisible. I like reading and drinking wine and cuddling on the couch while watching movies. I don't want to worry about saying the wrong thing or sending the entire palace into lockdown because I messed up some social decorum. Then there is the idea that people want me dead because of what I am. I can't change the fact I'm human."

"I can help you with all that," he said.

"Really? And I can trust you will tell me everything why? You didn't explain the whole dining hall thing to me tonight before abandoning me up there. And I seem to recall you telling me that the portal wouldn't take me home for another Earth year."

"It won't."

"That's not what your mother told me."

"I do not know what she said, but it will not take you back to your village for another year."

Jenna sighed. Now she was frustrated. "But it does go to Earth every night. You could take me back to another village. I have my wallet in my bag so I can make my way home."

All fight instantly drained out of him, and his hands dropped to his side. "Is that your wish?"

"Yes. No. Maybe." Jenna pushed her hands into her hair and pulled lightly at the roots, wishing the right answer would come to her. "I don't know. I didn't get my work turned in so I'm probably out of a job anyway. My rent is on auto pay from my bank account, so I have a little time. I don't know. I...I just don't know."

FEAR GRIPPED RAFE'S CHEST, and he knew what he had to do. If Jenna demanded he take her home, he would have no choice. He sat before her on the bed. "I agree to your dating terms. We will be all those things but not mated. But don't leave me."

How could she not know her heart was his? Frustration filled him with doubts. He was offering everything that he was, everything he had, his very life to her, and she didn't want it. She wanted him as a lover, and he would gladly go to her bed when commanded, but the notion left him hollow inside.

She wanted his body but not his love. He didn't breathe until she nodded her head in agreement.

"Dating is good," she said. "Very good. Thank you."

"As m'lady wishes." Rafe stood, moving to make the room darker so that they may sleep.

"You're not going to stay?"

"Yes, I will stay. My place is here with you." He pressed a button and the lights dimmed into darkness. His eyes shifted, seeing easily as he made his way back to the bed. He pulled at the covers she clutched to her chest, forcing her to release them. When he'd managed to settle her back into his arms, he whispered, "It is late. Rest. No harm will come to you this night."

THREE WEEKS, at least by Jenna's best estimate, had passed since she'd agreed to be Rafe's lover. She still had difficulty telling time since the sun—make that three suns—never set. At first it felt like an exotic vacation, a break from having to go to work, from having to worry about retirement plans and deadlines imposed by her boss. The only difference was this vacation wasn't ending. All the new and shiny was starting to be slightly oppressive. She hated to admit it because everyone was very kind to her, and they tried to please her.

Always tried to please her.

Jenna stared at the mountain of blue bread loaves pyramided on the chair cushion in her suite in contemplation before turning to the stack taking up most of her couch. Glancing at the fresh loaf in her hands, she grimaced. If she never saw another carb again in her life, it would be too soon.

"Come back to bed," Rafe ordered.

"This room smells like an old bakery," Jenna complained. She finally opted to take the newest loaf back to the bed with her. "What am I supposed to do with all this bread? I can't keep smuggling them to your chambers to throw pieces off your balcony. They bring me loaves faster than I can get rid of them. Are you sure there are no hungry poor people I can give them to?"

"I have told you, m'lady, everyone works and everyone eats. It is our way." Rafe grinned and held up the covers to show off his current erection. Though she didn't have proof, she was starting to suspect Var men had male erection drugs flowing through their veins. The man never seemed to tire. A few nights she'd had to protest to even get some sleep.

"You look hungry," she observed before throwing the loaf at him. He caught it but dropped the blanket in the process. "Here. Eat. I have run out of places to put them."

Rafe let his face partially shift so that he had fangs. Making a low growling noise, he bit fiercely into it and shook his head. A tiny shiver ran through

Jenna. He'd discovered how much she liked his little shows of shifter power. His face shifted back, and he began to chew. When he swallowed, he said, "Take off your clothes and come back to bed." He took another bite, this time less aggressively.

"Help me figure out a way to make the bread stop," Jenna said.

Rafe chuckled and took another bite.

"I'm glad you think this is funny because I expect you to keep eating until it's all gone." She gestured to the piles on the couch and mantel.

"You told the hall you liked blue bread," Rafe said. "The people wish to honor and please you."

Jenna had met several of "the people" and got the impression they really just wanted an excuse to talk to the new human. They kept staring and giggling and examining her. "I think they just want to have a good look at me and so use the bread as an excuse. What will happen if I just refuse to take it?"

Rafe sat up. "No, don't do that. You'll insult whoever brings it. If you wait, it will stop on its own."

"Then you better make room for it in your chambers because I'm about to start stacking it on your floor."

"You are always so serious," he said, not for the first time.

"And you are always not-so-serious," she answered. "Everything is a game."

"Only the best things." He gave her a steamy once over and grinned.

"Rafe, please, help, the bread." Jenna crossed her arms over her chest, but the gesture did little to dissuade his growing lust.

"I'll tell you how to make it stop, but you won't like it."

Looking around at the blue piles, she said, "I'll do anything."

"You'll have to be on display again. You told me you didn't want to have to do that."

"Display and then what?"

"Go to the dining hall with me and thank them for their generosity. Tell them how welcome and safe you feel here." Rafe grinned. "Perhaps mention you are ready to be my princess."

"Rafe..."

"What? The people want to love you. They see your kind heart and your open smile." He threw the bread over the foot of the bed toward the couch. It bounced over the floor. This time he tossed the covers completely off his naked body. His eyes flashed with gold as he silently beckoned her to go to him.

Her logical brain tried to protest, but her body obeyed him. Jenna crawled onto the bed before leaning over to kiss the center of his chest. She felt his heart beat against her lips.

"I do like some of your games," she whispered. "I don't try to always be serious."

"There is one game I have been thinking about that we haven't done," he said.

"Really?" She couldn't help falling for his magnetic spell. From that first instant she'd felt his pull. Endless hours of sex had yet to ease her attraction. In fact, if she were honest, discovery of him and his passions only made her want him more. All he had to do was drown her in kisses, and she was bending to his sexual will. If he wanted her bent over, she bent over. If he urged her to ride, she climbed on his lap. If he needed his cock sucked he'd often get her into the shower like the first time. If he woke up restless in the middle of the night and found his way to kiss between her thighs, she had no choice but to climax against his lips and tongue. That last one seemed to be a favorite since he did it often. He seemed to enjoy it when she was disorientated with sleep and jerking incoherently.

"This pied piper you mentioned to me when you first arrived. I would like to know what it is."

Jenna laughed and teased, "I don't think you're ready for that."

"But, I am strong and virile. I am ready to do as you command," he assured her.

She debated on whether or not to tell him it simply had to do with his magnetic eyes pulling her in and not some sexual feat. "I was teasing. It only means you are so attractive you are like a lure to women."

"Lure?"

"Trap. Like a hunter drawing in his prey," she said.

Rafe grinned and surprised her by jumping out of the bed. He hurried to the lights and made the room dark. Seconds later, she could hear him growling and the sound of claws hitting the stone floor as he moved. A tiny shiver of anticipation filled her as she tried to follow his movements.

She squinted but couldn't see him in the dark. "Rafe, this isn't what I meant. What are you doing?"

The low growl answered her, rumbling dangerously in the back of his throat in the opposite direction that she thought he was in. She gave a small gasp of surprise. Her heartbeat quickened as she waited for him to pounce, not knowing where it would come from.

"Rafe?" she whispered.

Another growl sounded in a different location, and then another.

She burrowed into the covers to her neck, leaving only her face and ears out. Suddenly, a loud roar sounded and he pounced. Rafe landed on her legs. Jenna screamed, startled.

Light suddenly burst forth from the door as two guards ran inside, half shifted and ready to fight. "M'lady!" She was pinned beneath the covers. Rafe straddled her with his human body. When the guards saw the naked prince, they instantly backed away. "Forgive us, we thought..."

The rest of what they said was lost as they closed the door.

"Oh, no..." Jenna rocked, trying to free herself. She couldn't believe they'd just been walked in on.

Rafe laughed. He leaned over, letting her have a little more wiggle room beneath the cage of blankets. "I think it is you who is not ready to be pipered. Though you are very lovely prey."

"And I can't believe you let the guards hear you!" She squirmed harder.

"I have explained the shifter hearing to you, right?" His lips brushed her cheek.

"Yes, but...oh, I see." Jenna closed her eyes tight

and made a weak noise. "So you're saying with shifter hearing they can always hear what we're doing in here and..."

"They won't listen. It would be impolite," Rafe said. She felt him smile against her. He began working the covers down from her body before pulling on the underdress she used as a nightgown.

"This is so embarrassing." Now that her arms were freed, she pushed at his chest. "Get up."

He let her push him up, but only so that he could press his hips forward. His arousal moved over her stomach. "What if I promise to be quiet?"

"I can't, not knowing they might be..."

Rafe took her hands and pinned them above her head. He threaded his leg between hers and kneed one of her legs open before moving to do the same to the other side. When she was spread open, he drew his hips to hers.

"I've captured my prey," he whispered, "and now I'm going to stake claim."

He thrust himself inside her. As it always did, her body readily accepted him.

"Rafe..."

He stretched along her length, holding her wrists over her head. One of his knees bent into hers as he moved sensually against her body to thrust. "Now, do you want to pretend to fight me off, little prey?"

Instantly understanding his game, she tugged at her wrists. The movement caused him to slide in deep and press down. Liking it, she fought harder, careful not to cry out. Rafe moaned. She managed to buck up, and his erection slipped out.

With a low growl, he flipped her onto her stomach and held her down as he entered her from behind. The position wasn't deep enough, so he drew her back to get better leverage. Holding her by her hips, his thrusts became frantic as he claimed her. The mattress pressed hard to her chest, and she gasped for breath. Pleasure came hard and sure. She forgot to keep quiet as she cried out her climax. Rafe's animalistic release met hers and he locked is hips to her ass.

When finally he let go, she collapsed forward and didn't move. Every nerve tingled, and her bones felt as if they melted out of her skin.

He fell to the mattress beside her. "I like this piper game. Perhaps next time we'll play it in the forest."

18

"Thank you for your generosity in welcoming me to your home world." Jenna smiled her frozen smile at the crowd. This was everything nightmares were made of—public speaking while standing in a medieval lady's gown, all eyes examining her to pass judgment, all ears listening to her every word.

The queen had seen to it gowns were made to fit Jenna, which was to say the gowns were made to the queen's liking. A snug red bodice flowed into a floor length skirt. An embroidered braid wrapped the neckline, went straight down the front only to wrap around the hemline. A contrasting green and gold belt hung low on her hips but was more decorative than functional. A smaller version of the belt had been made into a headband. Apparently the queen was very excited by the fact the dress looked lovely with her red hair. Lovely is not the word Jenna would have used. Now, if she were in the market to date Santa Claus, the red and green Christmas theme would have been perfect.

When no one moved, she looked to Rafe, who stood by her side. The rest of his family lined up next to them at the head table. She leaned to him and whispered, "I said it. Now what?"

"Tell them you're my princess," he answered just as quietly, giving her a playful grin.

"Rafe," she scolded in a hush. "Be serious."

"I am serious." His eyes dipped to her mouth, and she felt her cheeks heating under his gaze.

"Rafe," she mouthed in warning, well aware of everyone watching them.

"Bow your head and take your seat," he whispered.

Jenna bowed her head and sat. The gathered pounded their applause onto the tabletop. The royal family also took their seats, and the servants began to bring food. Jenna took a deep breath and held it, trying to calm her nerves. At least it was over. No more blue bread. No more speeches.

A guard approached the king and spoke to him in their native tongue. The king glanced up to the ceiling before answering with a curt nod. Ivar leaned over his mother to join the conversation.

"You look lovely," Rafe said, not for the first time.

"I'm just glad the hard part is over," she answered. A servant set slices of blue bread before her on the table. Jenna made a weak noise. When the woman was out of earshot, she said, "You have to be joking."

Rafe chuckled. "It has nothing to do with you. We're having a traditional yorkin dish, which is customarily served with bread."

"We have guests landing," the king said when the guard retreated the way he'd come. "Syog vessel."

"I am not doing the negotiations," Ivar stated.

"Don't look to me," the queen said. "I don't have the right equipment."

"Who are the Syog?" Jenna asked.

"They're a very aggressive alien," Rafe paused as if considering his words, before adding, "with a particular fondness for uncomfortable negotiations."

Ivar laughed. "You could say that."

"Just don't agree to negotiate anything with them." Rafe's hand brushed against her leg. "It does not end well."

"Stop that," she whispered, pulling her leg away from him.

"Stop what?" He smiled his rakishly handsome smile but lifted his hand back to the tabletop. Servants brought the yorkin dish. It smelled and looked like peppery sirloin steak and was cut into bite size chunks.

"How many aliens are there?" she asked.

"I could not begin to count the population of all alien species." Rafe lifted a two prong fork and stabbed a piece of meat.

"You know what I mean. How many species are there?"

"I could not begin to count how many species of aliens are out there. We meet new ones all the time," Rafe said.

"Twenty-three have visited this planet so far," Ivar answered. "And there is an accounting of at least three times as many."

"So many." Jenna lifted her fork. "Do they look mostly like we do? Or do they look like Roswell and Mogul?"

"I have not seen any that look like the Reticulans," Ivar said before Rafe could tease her again with a non-answer. "Many are what are known as humanoid, as are Earth people, as are Var and Draig. The Syog are humanoid."

"Do they shift?" she asked.

"They—" Ivar began.

"Rafe, you should bring Lady Jenna up to meet them since she is so curious," the queen said.

Rafe didn't readily answer. He also turned his back on her to face his mother so she couldn't see his face. "Did the guard say which ship it was?"

Ivar smiled. Jenna was sure she'd never seen the man look mischievous before. It was a little unsettling.

"Just a ship," the queen said.

"It's decided. Rafe will greet the Syog," the king said. "And be nice to them. We need all the alien allies we can get."

19

Jenna watched in stunned horror as two very symmetrically perfect athletic alien supermodels wrapped their arms around Rafe and refused to let him go. The landing pad stretched along the rooftop with white stones inlaid into the red to mark where the ships were to land. At first she'd been mesmerized to see a spaceship up close and had been full of questions about flight and ships and space travel. That was until the alien babes sauntered across the pad like they were on a runway.

And now they were groping Rafe.

Every insecurity ever known to non-supermodel women rose up inside her. It was bad enough Jenna felt like a walking Mrs. Claus minus the bonnet, but the two supermodels looked like science fiction

Roman gladiators in barbaric bikinis. Behind them stood three very beautiful men, also fantasy gladiator types, also perfectly muscled.

Out of the crowd gathering on the rooftop, she really didn't look like she belonged. Jenna wrapped her arms across her waist. She didn't need to speak Syog in order to understand what the women were saying. If their hands roaming Rafe's chest and their sultry expressions were to be believed, they had been lovers in the past and wished to rekindle the relationship.

Rafe took their hands and pressed them away from him. He turned to motion to her in introduction. She understood "Lady Jenna" but nothing else. The women stared at her until Jenna glanced away first, whispered to each other, and then laughed.

"You look like you have catching up to do," Jenna said to Rafe. "I'm going to let you," she glanced over the women. "Well, I know how eager you are to negotiate."

Rafe stiffened. The women smiled. The Syog men stepped forward.

Jenna didn't wait around to watch more groping.

Rafe had to stop himself from chasing after Jenna. If he left now the Syog would take it as a sign of disrespect and interpret it as a challenge. They were not the most intelligent species, but what they lacked in wit, they more than made up in brute force and sexual conquests. In the past, Rafe had enjoyed the rough games Takka and Kakka played. Now he wondered what he'd ever seen in them. They were vapid, hollow shells when compared to the great beauty and brains of his Jenna.

"We wish you to allow one of our warriors to learn from yours." Kommo was the leader and Takka's brother. At least, that's what Rafe had always assumed from the broken conversations of Syog and Var that they managed to have.

"If I agree there is no need to negotiate," Rafe said, already flinching at the idea.

Kommo lifted a semi-protective metal plate and extended it to Rafe. "Then I wish to leave two warriors."

Rafe knew from experience there was no way of getting around negotiations. They would keep making demands until Rafe had no choice but to refuse their request and gave in. He took the plate and secured it over his hips like a codpiece. "Let's get this over with."

20

JENNA PACED HER ROOM, thinking of Rafe being touched by those women. Jealousy surged through her. Damn him for making her jealous. Damn those women for touching him. Damn her for the impulse to go and stake claim to Rafe. Her heart physically ached.

What had happened to her? She was never this insecure. She was happy with the way she looked, confident in her intellect.

She pulled the green headband off her head before unlatching the low belt. She threw them on the bed. Restless, she continued to pace. Her hand ran over the remote cat. The television turned on. As if to mock her, a black and white starlet danced on stage, wiggling her feathered butt. Jenna promptly turned it off.

Where was Rafe? What was he doing?

The image of the two Syogs caressing him fueled her annoyed thoughts. She should never have left him alone. She should have grabbed him and staked some sort of claim. She should have punched those grabby bitches in their pretty faces.

She paced faster. Hearing a squish beneath her toes, she froze and looked down. She'd stepped on the edge of the queen's gray rug monster, Tog-tog. Jenna hopped back. "Dammit, why are you on the floor again?"

The flat fur began to shake violently. It made a strange, angry grumble, like an earthquake about to erupt.

"What are you doing? Tog-tog?" Jenna slowly backed away toward the door. "Easy, carpet. It was an accident. I didn't mean to..."

The shaking creature started to expand. The noise became louder, and she swore she felt the vibrations running up her legs from the stone floor. Once it was inflated, instead of running on its six short legs, it rolled toward her like an oversized bowling ball, pushing off its legs with every rotation to gain speed.

Jenna leaped out of the way. The creature crashed into the side of the couch and re-angled to try again. She didn't wait around to see what would happen when it managed to knock her over. The door swung open, and she ran through it, right into Hector. The guard tried to steady her, but Jenna pushed him back and slammed the suite door shut behind her. Tog-tog slammed against the wood so hard she worried it might crack. Breathing deeply, she eyed Hector as they waited and listen. Another crash sounded on the far side of the room.

"M'lady?" Hector asked, looking her over before staring at the suite door.

"Lesson learned." She gave a nervous laugh. "Don't accidently step on the Tog-tog."

Another crash sounded. The television turned on, the volume loud. And there went the remote control cat statue.

"I should probably not go back in there," she said. Then, patting Hector lightly on the arm. "Thanks for the rescue."

Hector looked at where she touched him and then around the hall. It wasn't a secret she was Prince Rafe's lover. No wonder her touch made the man uncomfortable. Jenna turned to leave.

"Wait," Hector ordered. "You are not to be unescorted."

"Oh, it's fine," she said. "Prince Rafe is negotiating with aliens and I'm going to join him." She again made a move to go to the stairwell leading up.

"Prince Rafe is in the forest. If you insist on seeing him, I will take you. I cannot let you out of my sight, or I will be punished."

"Very well," Jenna nodded. "I wouldn't want you punished."

"M'lady is very kind," Hector answered. When Jenna tried to move toward the stairwell that would lead her down to the front entrance, he stopped her by saying, "Follow me."

They moved in the other direction.

"The palace is quiet," she observed as they neared the balcony. A cool breeze swept along the walkway, fluttering the gauze sunblocks inward. Their feet echoed as they walked.

"Everyone is watching the negotiations," Hector said.

"Watching?" Jenna stopped walking. Unbidden the image of Rafe with two Syog beauties came to mind, and she scowled. "What exactly is there to watch?"

"M'lady..." Hector gestured for her to walk, and

she obeyed. "The Syog are known to be very aggressive negotiators. I'm surprised Prince Rafe mentioned the word to them."

"The Syog are very pretty. I'm sure they're popular with the locals," Jenna allowed, hating the words even as she said them. Jealousy again filled her until she could barely focus on Hector's back.

"Some seem to think so." He led her to the tower and pressed a stone. A hidden entryway opened, and he stepped inside. Jenna hesitated before going into the darkened stairwell. It wound downward.

"I have never been in the towers," Jenna said as she moved to follow him. The stone entry closed as they walked away, sealing them in.

"Not many aliens have," he said. "They are used for castle defense and communication."

"I thought the king and queen lived in them." She placed her hand on the wall and followed the sound of his feet.

"Only in one."

"Are we almost there?" Jenna quickened her pace to keep up with him. "I know it's several stories, but it seems like we're going down too far."

"Yes, almost, can't you see the markings?"

"It's too dark. I can't see anything," Jenna said.

"...inferior," Hector mumbled.

"I'm sorry?"

"Human eyesight is inferior," he said louder.

Jenna stopped walking. She took a hesitant step back up the way they'd come.

"Come on," he ordered.

"I think I'm going to go back up. I'm sure Tog-tog has calmed down by now."

"Come," he said again. "There is nothing to fear in the dark."

"He likes it when I play with him," she lied. Jenna backed away faster.

"Accursed humans," Hector growled. Jenna tripped, flailing her arms when she felt him grab for her. He managed to capture her wrist and used it to drag her down the stairwell behind him. Her feet tripped but he didn't seem to care if she walked or if she slid her way down. "Bad senses. Bad instincts. Can't even see in the dark. And they think Earth women are the answer to saving the shifter blood-lines? All you'll do is weaken us."

"Hector, please. I haven't done anything to you, or to the Nutef. That's what you are, isn't it? A Nutef?" Her body slammed into the wall at his hard tug and then she fell forward, hitting his back. He growled, pushing her off him while still jerking her arm. She bounced and stumbled.

Finally, he stopped, and the stone opened into a small cave. The exit was shaded by vines that fluttered into the forest. When she turned, all that was left of the tower entryway was foundation stones covered in yellowish-green moss.

"Hector," Jenna said, trying to sound calm. "It's not too late. We can go back."

"Do you think I like having to leave my post? Do you think I like having to disobey the orders of my king? I have been a loyal guard for centuries. I love my people. That is why I do this. It is too late to stop this. You should never have come to where you don't belong." Hector pulled her toward the cave exit. "I don't want to kill you, Lady Jenna. You are kind for a human, but you are still human. We cannot let a human become princess. You cannot taint the most sacred of our bloodlines."

"Our fathers should not have given the portal to the dragon. Our fathers should have stopped it when King Ainmire took the alien Lassairfhina as his bride and made her queen. They told themselves the king knew best. They told themselves she was beautiful and from a noble alien people. They told themselves lies, and they opened the door for human women." The words came from outside the cave, rising with loud conviction. "We know what must be done. If we stay vigilant, sooner or later they will stop bringing humans through the portals. If enough humans are sacrificed, they will see the will of the gods. They will know the people do not want tainted blood. My son, Myrddin, will know many Var wives, as my father, Lord Myrddin claimed my Var mother. As too will your sons and daughters be Var. Let my family be an example. We are the oldest. We are Old House Nobles. We are Var."

Hector pushed Jenna outside, and she fell to the ground. Almost instantly, she was on her feet. Her heart pounded in fear as cheering sounded. Over a dozen men stood in the clearing in brown robes. Hoods covered their heads affixed to flat wooden masks over their face. The bottoms of the masks were sharpened points tipped with metal, symbolic of the top row of a cat's fangs. Eye holes had been cut but were so deep the color of the eyes beneath were shaded in darkness.

"You bring honor, Hector," the speaker declared. Clearly the leader, he stood before the others on an outcropping of stone. Long black hair showed from beneath his hood to stand against his chest.

"Thank you, Lord Myrddin," Hector said.

Clawed hands poked out from the long sleeves of the robes. They were shifted into cat-men underneath. Orange fur. White fur. Striped hands. Golden fur. Black…

Jenna's eyes swept up to the man with black fur on his hands. Was he the one who tried to harm her in the shower?

Jenna tried to follow Hector. "Hector, please, don't do this."

"I am sorry, m'lady. This is about more than you or I." Hector disappeared back into the cave. She heard stone move to let him pass into the tower's base.

"I'll leave," she said. "Just tell me how to get to the portal and I'll go."

Low growls sounded as an answer. Myrddin spoke to them in their native language, passionately growling and pointing at her.

"I don't understand," Jenna protested. She made a move to run, but a follower blocked her path. "I didn't do anything to you."

"You spread your legs for the prince," the leader said. "There can only be one way to ensure you do not taint the blood."

"But I'm not pregnant," Jenna insisted. "We have doctors that give us medicine to prevent pregnancy. There is no tainted blood here. We're all good."

"Good?" The leader laughed at her. He turned to

his followers. "We made a mistake when we tried to take Princess Eve through the portal to kill her. The gods were angry at our shame in our actions. They want all to know our conviction. This time the sacrifice will be seen. We will not wait. We will stand strong and proud. We will show them our actions. All will know. The sacrifice will be now."

Low growls sounded only to rise and fall, repeating in a rhythmic pattern, crescendoing and subsiding in waves of sound. Their chant ended all conversation. The leader reached behind to the stone and tossed long coils of rope down to his followers. Four of the men came toward her. Jenna scurried out of the way, ready to run. Within seconds, two others had her captured between them. She screamed, and they stuck a robed arm into her mouth to shut her up. She bit down. Another arm wrapped her neck, choking her. Jenna clawed at the arms to be free, but became dizzy when the hold tightened against her neck.

Blackness threatened, and she lost some of her ability to fight. She felt a tug on her wrists, then on her ankles. They bared her feet. Her arms were drawn to the side by rope shackles.

"The gods will know our loyalty," the leader yelled.

The chanting stopped as the men cheered. The hold on her head released, but before she could find enough breath to scream a rope gag replaced the arm. The coarse material dug into her sensitive lips and chafed her delicate skin.

They jerked her arms violently, and she was hoisted several feet off the ground to hang. Someone pulled at the rope tied around her head, and she was forced to look up at the sky. Her legs were stretched wide until she hung like an X from the tree limbs. Instantly her arms ached from the position, feeling as if they might rip from her body.

Hot tears streamed down her face. Someone grabbed her foot, and she tried to wiggle free. White heat tore into the sole of her foot as they sliced her open. Anticipating what was to come, she kicked harder when they grabbed her other foot. She screamed into the rope gag before coughing for breath. Blood ran down the soles of her feet to her toes.

The men circled around her, chanting once more. The sound washed over her, a demonic reality she could not escape.

Rafe, dammit, you promised to keep me safe, she thought, willing someone to come and save her and knowing they would not know where to find her.

Rafe limped down the stairs, cupping his sore manhood. The sensitive flesh of his inner thighs felt bruised, but that was nothing to the gut-wrenching ache in his testicles. Had he not seen Kommo doubled over in pain after Rafe planted his foot between the Syog's legs, Rafe would have thought the aliens lacked humanoid equipment.

Ivar chuckled to see his brother. "Ball racking negotiations over already? I thought you would have lasted at least three kicks this time."

"I hate you," Rafe said. "You knew they wanted something from us, didn't you? You sent me on purpose. You told Jenna to say the word negotiation. I don't know how or when, but you did."

"I thought Jenna would enjoy the show. I'm sure

you've done something to her at some point to deserve it," Ivar said. Then, looking behind Rafe, he asked, "Where is Lady Jenna?"

"I'm going to find her now. She left before the negotiation started. I sent a few of the guards to look for her and bring her back to her suite until I could talk to her." Rafe limped his way toward the stairwell. Ivar took pity on him and offered an arm to help him down. As they neared the suite, a loud crash caught their attention.

Rafe ignored his pain as he ran toward her room. Ivar was faster and thrust open the door first. Seconds later, Ivar came flying out with a round gray fur ball in his gut. He slammed into the hallway wall and crumpled to the floor. Tog-tog instantly relaxed and deflated a little so that he could scurry away down the hall.

Ivar clutched at his manhood, groaning. Rafe laughed, even though the jiggling hurt. "Serves you right."

"What the hell angered him?" Ivar asked, taking measured breaths as he came to his feet. He leaned over.

Rafe hurried into the room. "Jenna? Are you in here? Jenna?"

She wasn't there.

Rafe came out of the room. "Something is off. I feel it."

"She is probably hiding from Tog-tog. Come, we'll find her in the dining hall," Ivar said.

"No, I'm telling you. I feel she is in danger," Rafe forgot his own pain as he trusted his emotions to guide him. He raced through the hall.

"Rafe?" the queen demanded. "What did you do to Tog-t—"

"Jenna's in trouble," he yelled, sprinting past his mother. Rafe's fur sprouted over his features as he ran. Fangs elongated in his mouth and sharpened claws stretched from his fingertips.

"Jenna?" the queen repeated. She raced after her sons.

Rafe caught Jenna's scent and chased it. Hector emerged from the tower door. The scent led Rafe to the guard. He grabbed him and tossed him up against a wall, holding him off the ground. Hector half-shifted with golden fur and slashed a hand to defend himself. He hit Rafe's arm and drew blood.

Rafe slid him from the wall and slammed him into the floor. "Where is she?"

"Rafe!" Ivar commanded.

"I smell her on him," Rafe said. Anger rippled over him.

Hector lifted his hands over his face. "This is about more than you or I, my prince."

"Rafe, down here," Ivar ordered.

Rafe punched Hector so hard he knocked the cat-shifter out. To his mother, he said, "Don't let him go." He ran after his brother. "Do you hear her?"

"I smell fear and blood." Ivar jumped more than ran down the tower stairs so fast he needed to brace his hand against the wall to redirect his descent.

Rafe did the same. He too smelled blood. It was faint and the amount too little to be more than a cut, but combined with the tinge of fear it was enough. He had never felt so scared in all his days. He imagined he heard her in his head calling to him, crying out his name.

Ivar stopped at the bottom. Rafe nearly crashed into him. His brother motioned for silence as he reached for the stone.

The smell of blood became more intense as the entrance opened. Low chants sounded. Ivar grabbed Rafe's arm before he surged forward into danger. Rafe snuck through the cave to peer through the vines. He focused his senses. The sound of dripping liquid reverberated off the forest floor. When he leaned to the side, he detected Jenna's bloody foot. She didn't move. His heart stopped beating.

"Don't leave me," he whispered.

Her foot twitched.

Rafe growled, charging to face whoever held her. It didn't matter that a dozen Nutef followers surrounded her. It could have been a hundred soldiers, and he would have run into battle. Rafe hit his first target, breaking the man's limb before launching his body at a robed tiger shifter. His claw snagged a mask, and he whipped a shifter around by his face right into a tree.

"Rafe, knife," Ivar shouted. His brother fought three of Jenna's attackers. Rafe saw a flash of silver and dodged the blade. The scent of Jenna's blood followed the knife, and he grabbed the wrist. Bringing his knee up he slammed the blade hand down hard.

"I hate the tower steps. I can never find the door stone," the queen's voice came from inside the cave. She emerged only to yell, "To ground!"

Rafe and Ivar instantly dove onto the ground. The attackers looked confused as they turned defensively toward the queen. Intense heat radiated from their angry mother. Rafe glanced up in time to seek her skin ignite with red flames. The fire shot from her body, spreading over the attackers. Cat-shifters screamed as they burned. The queen turned her body, hitting the man on the outcropping. The Nutef leader tried to jump out of the way, but the queen followed him, concentrating her heat until he stopped screaming.

Rafe felt his skin sizzle. Queen Lassairfhina pulled the flames back into her body and convulsed. She dropped to her knees. Rafe rolled to tamp out any fire burning his clothes from his back. When he stood, Ivar had pulled his shirt off and was draping it over their naked mother. She'd burned off her clothes.

Rafe found the bloody ceremonial knife in a charred hand. He took the hot blade, not caring that the hilt burned his skin. He cut Jenna's legs free.

"Help him," the queen ordered.

"Rafe, the blade," Ivar commanded.

Rafe tossed the knife to his brother. As Ivar cut the rope holding Jenna's arms, Rafe reached up to catch her as she fell. Ivar quickly moved to cut the last limb free. Jenna's eyelids drooped as she tried to focus on him.

"Don't try to talk," Rafe whispered. He wasn't sure if she could hear him or understand what he was saying. "You're safe now. I felt you. They can't hurt you. Not anymore." He cradled her in his arms.

"She really is your mate," the queen said.

"The medical bed," Ivar ordered. "I will stay here and make sure the flames don't reignite to burn down the forest."

"Of course she's my mate," Rafe whispered. "It's what I've been telling everyone all along."

He rushed Jenna into the cave.

"Ivar, you'll have to help me up the stairs to the dining hall. This just won't do," the queen complained to her oldest son, flapping her arms as she drowned in the material of Ivar's tunic shirt. She'd become a bony slip of a thing, the round plumpness of her figure having melted away. "I lost all my fuel."

"We could have taken them ourselves," Ivar answered, clearly not feeling sorry for her. The sound of tapping punctuated his words as he put out residual fires.

"What fun is that for me?" the queen returned. "Besides, no one threatens a child of mine without getting a taste of my wrath. All I know is Rafe better officially claim that girl soon, or I'm going to show him what a real fire—"

The sound of the tower entrance opening drowned out the rest of their conversation.

SHE IS SAFE. *She is safe.*

Rafe's mind repeated the same phrase over and over as if the thought would somehow make it all the more true. She'd been so limp in his arms when he carried her to the medical bed. As the machine worked, Rafe became all the more convinced that the gods had a hand in his life. They brought him to Jenna. She injured herself, and they brought the Reticulans to heal her. Ivar witnessed the technology and had the forethought to negotiate for equipment. That equipment was saving her.

Rafe was meant to meet her.

He was meant to love her.

They were fate.

Rafe looked at his clothing tainted with her blood. And he'd failed to protect her. He did not deserve to have her. Perhaps that is why she'd continually resisted marrying him. She knew from the very beginning what he didn't. He was not worthy of her.

For that, he must let her go.

JENNA JERKED AWAKE, trying to sit up. She bumped her head and then her hands on a low barrier. Struggling in her prison of plastic and bright light, she slid her arms and legs around trying to find a way out.

"Easy, Jenna." Rafe's voice sounded muffled.

"My feet burn," she answered, trying to kick away the heat and unable to. She managed to pull her arms over her chest and banged them on the plastic dome. "Get me out of this tanning bed."

"Not yet, it's healing you," Rafe answered.

"Healing?" Jenna gasped as the rush of what happened came over her. "Oh, no, Rafe, be careful Hector is one of them. He took me. And there was another, a man they called Myrddin with black hair. He has a son named Myrddin and his dad is named Myrddin."

"Yes. They're not a very imaginative bunch when it comes to names, the Myrddin men," Rafe said.

"Rafe, be serious!" Jenna found a seam in the bed and tried to wiggle her fingers into it in the hopes of prying it open.

"I am very serious. We got him," Rafe assured her. "Now let the medical bed work. The panel says you are to stop moving."

"There are more. I tried to remember. Gold fur, black fur, stripes, orange—" Her fingers met cooler air. "They wear wooden masks with metal tips on the bottom edge."

"You are safe. Everyone is safe. Those who threatened you are dead. The queen burned off all her clothes trying to save you and... Jenna, the panel says that you—*sacred cats*, woman, are you trying to escape?" Rafe touched her hand. She knew it was him because her body recognized his. Instead of holding her, he tried to stuff her fingers back inside. "Stop that, woman. You're not coming out until you're done."

"You make me sound like a cinnamon roll baking," she grumbled.

"I don't know what that is, but if it keeps you in there, that is exactly what you are. A cinnamon roll."

MICHELLE M. PILLOW

"Don't you dare start calling me that," Jenna warned.

"Now I want to," he playfully answered. Then, sounding more serious, he said, "I will make you a deal. If you stay in there, I will call you whatever you like."

The burning in her feet began to lessen, and she was starting to feel much better. Her neck muscles unclenched like the end of a fabulous massage. Jenna moaned with the relief of it.

"Jenna?" Rafe asked.

"I said deal," she answered, closing her eyes. "Let this cinnamon roll bake."

Jenna drifted in and out of sleep, pretty sure she'd discovered nirvana. The medical bed fixed things she didn't even know were wrong. Her eyeballs felt massaged. A slightly irritating ingrown toenail that barely bothered her went away.

"Stupid humans kept asking for anal probing," she mumbled. "They should have held out for this."

"Jenna?" Rafe asked. "How do you feel?"

"I'm never coming out," she answered, smiling and moaning in contentment.

"You have been in there for hours. It says it has finished."

The lid began to lift, and she tried to stop it. "No, I'm going to live in here."

"Jenna, come on, let me carry you to bed." Rafe pulled the lid up.

Jenna pouted her lip. "No. Tog-tog messed up my room, and it smells like stale bread in there." She started to reach for the lid and then paused. "I might have misheard, but did you say the queen burned off her clothes? Is she hurt?"

Rafe reached in to cup her cheek. "Yes, she did. No, she is not injured. I will explain it all later."

"So, ah, did the queen burn off my clothes too?" Jenna glanced down at her naked body and gave a small laugh.

"That is how the bed works. You must—"

Jenna's smile faded as she saw the blood on his shirt. "You're hurt. Get in here." She pushed out of the bed and pulled on his shirt. "Get naked and get in that bed. Now."

"It's your blood." He put his hands on hers to stop her.

"Even better. Get naked and get in this bed with me." She grinned and nodded slowly. "This is a great idea."

His eyes turned down. Holding her hands in his,

he ran his thumb over her knuckles. "I need you to forgive me."

"Forgive you?" Jenna leaned over, trying to see his face. "What's going on here? Usually, I'm the one who is serious."

"I'm taking you back to Earth." He squeezed her hands gently and stood. "I'll have the servants bring your clothes." He made a move for the door.

Jenna pushed to her feet and wobbled on her overly relaxed muscles. "Don't you dare open that door. You can't just say vague things like that and then walk away. I will stumble after you naked if I have to."

Rafe faced her. The expression on his face broke her heart a little bit. "I didn't keep you safe. I said no harm would come to you here. I failed you. You deserve better."

"Give me your shirt," Jenna said, feeling vulnerable. She'd never seen him like this. He obeyed, handing her the shirt. Jenna slipped it over her head, not caring that it was stained with her blood. The material was infused with his heat and his smell. "Are you trying to break up with me?"

"Break you up?" When he walked his legs were spread a little too far apart, and he tried not to wince.

"What is this really about? You see your old girlfriends and decide marriage isn't for you, after all?" Jenna hugged her arms to her chest.

"Girlfriends?"

"The Syog women," Jenna stated, not sure if she wanted to yell at him, or cry, or maybe punch him in the nose and chase down a couple alien supermodels and punch them as well. "You spent some time with them and decided they were less trouble than I am?"

"You are a confusing woman," Rafe said. "I am trying to do the right thing by you."

"Is that what you call this? I can't believe you got me out of the medical tanning bed for this." She paced the small room.

"I did not enjoy my time with the Syog today. You called for a negotiation." He shifted his weight uncomfortably. "You didn't even stay to watch. You ran away, and I couldn't go after you because... It doesn't matter. I am still at fault. I did not keep you safe."

"I wasn't going to stand by to be laughed at," she said. "Or watch you grope each other."

"No one groped me," Rafe paused. "At least I don't think they did."

"Oh, they groped. They groped the hell out of you," Jenna quipped. "I think that's the real reason you want to get rid of me."

"I don't want to get rid of you."

"Well, you aren't trying to keep me. So what would you call this? One minute you're laughing at me and the next you want to throw me through the portal." Jenna tried not to breathe too deeply. The shirt smelled of him, and their arguing was heating her blood.

"No one laughed at you."

"Don't lie. You introduced me, and they started gossiping and whispering and laughing at me. You're embarrassed by me."

"Jenna," Rafe insisted. "No one laughed at you. They were laughing at me. I told them I had found love. They thought it was amusing since they had—"

"So you didn't sleep with them?"

"Only long before I met you," he said. "There is no one else for me, not since you walked into my life. Trust me when I say I did not enjoy being with the Syog today."

"Then why are you moving funny?" She glanced down at his crotch to emphasize her meaning.

"Negotiations." Rafe grimaced. "The Syog are brutal. They call it ball racking. Whoever can take the most kicks wins."

"You negotiated by kicking each other in the

balls?" Jenna flinched. "What kind of meathead frat boy nonsense is that?"

"That is why no one mentions negotiating when they are here," Rafe said. "They make good allies despite their customs. Those customs make them unlikable so if we can deal with them we guarantee a friendship. As of now no one wants to hurt us, but the idea of an alien attack is a real problem that must be planned for. Also, they could lead us to other aliens who will become our allies."

"I got you kicked in the balls?" Jenna pointed at the medical bed. "Get in the bed, Rafe."

"But—"

"This isn't up for discussion." She flicked her hand. "I said get in the bed."

Even as he reached for his waistband to undress, he said, "I don't want to fight with you."

"Then stop trying to get rid of me and get in the medical bed." Jenna gasped to see his bruised thighs. She grabbed his arms and helped him to lie down. "If you ever do something so stupid again I'll negotiate you myself."

"It looks worse than it is."

"I'm marrying an idiot," Jenna said as she pushed the lid down on top of him. It sealed shut, but she heard him bumping around on the inside.

"Jenna? What did you say?" he yelled.

"I said you're an idiot," Jenna answered loudly.

The monitor lit up and showed a blinking panel with different types of handprints. Seeing one with five fingers, she placed her hand on it. A light scanned her, and the panel said, "Human Earth welcome. Please wait. Scanning subject."

"Jenna?"

"I said I love you." She couldn't help but smile at the unit's lid as she imagined him inside.

"I marry you, too," he yelled. "And I love you, too."

A tiny shiver worked over her, and she felt heat running up and down her skin as if she felt what he was feeling on the inside. The sensation was so strong she placed her hand on the lid and felt that he did the same on the other side.

"What is that?"

"It is done. We have declared. You are my life mate, my wife. You can't be rid of me now."

"Wait a minute, that's it? We just say it? What about a wedding story? I take it back." She marched to the door. "Nope. Not happening now. I can't tell people I married you while you were getting your balls fixed after being stupid."

"Jenna, where are you going? Come back here,

woman. Sacred cats, you are frustrating. When the medical bed finishes and let's me out, we're going to speak about this."

"That's if you can find me, pied piper." Jenna smiled, shutting the door behind her, knowing as soon as he was free from the bed the hunter would be coming for his prey.

EPILOGUE

"Oh, my goodness, what are you wearing?" Jenna's eyes widened as she looked at her husband.

"A bet is a bet," Prince Finn stated. "And Rafe lost."

"My first trip back to Earth and you're going dressed as a prima ballerina?" Jenna covered her mouth and tried very hard not to laugh. The man really had no sense of modesty. "In a pink tutu and tights, no less."

Jenna wore the clothes she'd had on the day they met. Oddly, she had gotten used to dresses while living at the palace—after she'd became more vocal about how her dresses were made. No more Christmas colors and elaborate embroidery.

Rafe winked at her and turned to show his ass. "It looks good, right?"

"It looks something," Eve said, laughing. She stood next to her husband, the Draig heir prince, Kyran. The man gazed lovingly at his wife as if mesmerized by everything she said.

"At least your legs look—" Jenna began.

"Pink!" Eve interrupted. The women laughed harder.

"You are lucky your brother isn't here." Finn was the only single man going on the journey though he was mainly there to help carry whatever Jenna decided to take home.

Ivar was busy overseeing alien representatives who claimed to have invented a magical box that created food from molecules or some such science fiction nonsense, though they couldn't provide the actual box and merely wanted to gather recipes and food samples. For some reason, the king didn't want them telling the Draig about the frequency of alien visitors.

Rafe grinned at her. "You know I wear this because of you. Had you not been desperate to marry me at the diner I wouldn't have lost the bet."

"I thought she married you when you were

getting your balls fixed," Finn said. Jenna groaned. Everyone else laughed.

"You know, Finn, you should let us buy you some clothes while we're there tonight." Eve threaded her arm into Jenna's.

"We'll make sure everyone knows you're drag queen royalty," Jenna said, smiling. With men as sexy and confident—and a little too arrogant at times—as these shifters were, it was kind of a poetic justice that they kept telling Earth women they were "draqueens". Plus, it was funny. Eve and Jenna had no intention of correcting them.

"I'm not sure you'll feel so generous after you see the second half of the bet," Finn said.

"I'm not sure I want to know," Jenna bit her lip and eyed Rafe.

"Tonight, I must dance for you, my wife," Rafe said, giving a little twirl.

"And whoever else happens to be on the street at the time," Kyran added.

Jenna couldn't hold it in. She laughed so hard she gasped for breath. Eve joined her, and they nearly fell over.

"A bet is a bet," Finn repeated.

"Seriously, what was the bet over?" Jenna wiped the laughter tears from her eyes. "Unless your bet was to watch me knock myself out on a pole first, I know it wasn't about my following you home."

"He swore he would never give up his bachelor ways," Finn said.

"But then I saw you come into the diner, and I lost." Rafe reached for his wife. "So this is for you."

"You're lucky you're charming because I don't have a thing for men in tutus and leotards." Jenna leaned up for his kiss. The fluffy tulle pressed between them, and she couldn't help but start laughing again. She pulled back and said, "You better not get arrested in that thing because I promised the queen that I would use my money to buy movies and language books. I don't want to have to bail you out of jail instead."

Jenna touched her messenger bag. Inside were her apartment keys and wallet. It felt strange to be going home. The plan was to empty her bank account, buy supplies, and leave a note for her land-lord that she was vacating the apartment after gathering what belongings she wanted to keep. It made her sad to think no one on Earth would miss her.

As if sensing her small wave of sorrow, Rafe put his hands around her waist and pulled her close. When he looked at her, she still felt as if it was the first time, like his love for her was new and perfect and untainted. "I would wear a thousand tutus so long as I get to keep you."

"That sounded more romantic in your head, didn't it?" Jenna pressed her forehead to his and gazed into his eyes. "And I would wear a thousand tutus for you too."

"And nothing else?" Rafe grinned. "I will hold you to that, m'lady."

Jenna chuckled, knowing he would.

"Let's go already," Eve insisted, stepping up to the swirling purple light of the portal and kneeling to go in. The men had warned them that the other side of this particular portal trip was a tighter fit. "I am so hungry. I want cheeseburgers, and pie, and a pizza, and tacos, and ice cream, and—"

Finn pushed Eve into the portal, and she disappeared.

"Hey," Kyran growled at his brother before jumping in after his wife.

"That woman is obsessed with cheeseburgers." Finn stepped in and disappeared.

Now that they were alone, Rafe touched Jenna's cheek lovingly. "I am obsessed with you, my wife. I am sorry if tonight will be hard for you. I know you gave up an entire world to stay with me."

"Silly man," Jenna whispered. She wrapped her

arms around his neck and let her lips lightly brush against his. "Tonight is about tying up loose ends. *You* are my world. I don't need anything else. I have no regrets."

"I only have a single regret," he said, eyeing her hair. "That I will probably not be able to give you a daughter. I would have liked it very much to see her with hair and eyes like yours."

"I will take whatever fate has in store for us. I love you. That is what matters." Jenna knew someday they would have children but for now they enjoyed each other's company. According to the Var, when Jenna married Rafe their life force had combined and she would live as long as he. So they had hundreds of years to talk about babies.

"And I you, m'lady." Rafe closed the small distance between their lips and pulled her with him into the portal. As their bodies dissolved into a million little pieces to make the journey to Earth nothing mattered but that they were together.

The End

THE SERIES CONTINUES...

STRANDED WITH THE CAJUN

Captured by a Dragon-Shifter Book Three

The bayou is about to get a whole lot hotter for Drake. This alpha dragon-shifter had all but given up on finding a mate until one practically falls into his lap.

Prologue Excerpt

Two years ago...

Once a decision was made, it needed to remain made.

Dimosthenis had given this decision a lot of consideration. With his brother's death, he was the only remaining son to carry on the family bloodline.

Unfortunately, to do that, he needed to leave everything behind and travel to Earth.

A mate wasn't easy to find on his planet of Qurilixen. He loved his home, the shadowed marshes where he grew up, the trees near the borderlands so thick they could have been walls, the mountains where he now stood on the precipice of his future. However, for as beautiful as it was, there was something darker beneath the surface, a curse.

The Draig people were dying. Not with disease or war, but because their population lacked females. With no women, there were no babies. He was part of an entire generation of dragon-shifter men who had no wives. Well, all but one—a prince. The royal family had opened the portal to Earth in order to find wives for themselves. They guarded it jealously and did not let commoners go through. He was sure they had their reasons, reasons that made sense to the rulers, but for the everyday man who spent lonely night after night without the comfort of a wife, it was particularly cruel. Dimosthenis deserved a chance to have a family, a wife, love.

He deserved a trip through the portal.

The porous black rocks of the cave held his future. He'd followed the human Princess Eve and her escort down the hidden stairwell from inside the palace, careful to stay out of sight, and now hid by the cave's exterior exit for his chance to go in. All he had to do was step inside the darkness. He may never get another opportunity. There were those shifter factions who wanted to seal the portals forever, who didn't think human women were the answer. They had plans to detonate the hidden chamber.

If he left, he could never come home.

If he stayed, he might never find a mate.

A soft purple glow lit the cave. They must have activated the portal. He crept forward to watch from the shadows. Dragons and cats were carved into the stone chamber, pointing away from the portal, a symbol of their exodus from Earth. The elders told campfire stories of the portal's magic, of how it brought them from Earth, away from the persecution of human warlords. Had the humans changed? Or were the horror stories of hunting and slaughtering dragons still an Earth reality? Surely not every dragon and cat-shifter on Earth came through the portal, many yes, but there was no way of knowing how many chose to stay behind.

Fear filled him. There was no guarantee that love awaited him on the other side of the portal. In fact, it might only be death. Earth could be an ugly place. It could be filled with dragon-hating hunters. It could bring him nothing but loneliness and pain. Perhaps there was a reason the royals did not invite commoners through. Maybe he should listen to what the elders said, to the will of the gods as translated for him, and go home to wait for a blessing that may never come.

No. He had to try. He had left goodbye messages for his friends. The decision he made in this moment determined the rest of his life. To stay meant being alone forever, which was as good as deciding to die today. So there was no choice. He would jump into the unknown.

Updated Reading List and Links here: MichellePillow.com

ABOUT MICHELLE M. PILLOW

New York Times & *USA TODAY*
Bestselling Author

Michelle loves to travel and try new things, whether it's a paranormal investigation of an old Vaudeville Theatre or climbing Mayan temples in Belize. She believes life is an adventure fueled by copious amounts of coffee.

Newly relocated to the American South, Michelle is involved in various film and documentary projects with her talented director husband. She is mom to a fantastic artist. And she's managed by a dog and cat who make sure she's meeting her deadlines.

For the most part she can be found wearing pajama pants and working in her office. There may or may not be dancing. It's all part of the creative process.

**Come say hello! Michelle loves talking
with readers on social media!**

www.MichellePillow.com

facebook.com/AuthorMichellePillow

x.com/michellepillow

instagram.com/michellempillow

bookbub.com/authors/michelle-m-pillow

goodreads.com/Michelle_Pillow

amazon.com/author/michellepillow

youtube.com/michellepillow

pinterest.com/michellepillow

COMPLIMENTARY EXCERPTS

WANT MORE VAR?

LORDS OF THE VAR SERIES

Meet the future Var royals...
Shape-shifter Romance

The cat-shifter princes were raised to not believe in love, especially love for one woman, and they will do everything in their power to live up to their father's expectations. Oh, how the mighty will fall.

Lords of the Var® **Series**
The Savage King
The Playful Prince
The Bound Prince
The Rogue Prince
The Pirate Prince

Note: The *Lords of the Var*® series is set in the distant future and is part of the original Dragon Lords universe of series. To learn more, visit: michellepillow.com

PERFECT PRINCE

BY MICHELLE M. PILLOW

Want more Draig?

Dragon Lords Series

A Perfect Escape...

Nadja Aleksander has everything she could ever want in life, except her freedom. Skipping out on her engagement, to a man her controlling father has chosen for her, Nadja books passage on the first spaceship she can find. Bound for a planet of primitive humanoid males, Nadja plans on finding a simple, hardworking man who will allow her to live out her days in total obscurity.

A Perfect Mistake...

Dragon-shifter Prince Olek is pleased with his

refined and blushing bride. When she chooses him to be her life mate, appearing happy in her decision, his heart soars—until the next morning when his new princess wants nothing to do with him. Olek doesn't know what he's done to upset his alluring bride, but he is determined to reignite the hot sparks that burned the night they met.

Perfect Prince Excerpt

"Come, bride."

Again, she couldn't deny him, moving to dip under the green tent flap he held up for her. When she drew near him, she smelled the warm oil on his glistening skin. It mixed with the natural scent of him. She breathed deeply. This was as close as she had ever been to such an inadequately dressed man before.

She faltered in her movements, glancing up into his eyes. Before she knew what was happening, a strong hand was on her face, gently cupping her cheek. The touch was fire to her already flushed features. Her lips parted with a ragged, scared gasp.

Olek took it as an invitation and dipped his head forward.

Nadja almost screamed when he tried to kiss her. Her first reaction was to run. Dodging under his arm, she darted inside the tent. Nadja froze mid-step as she looked around. The red earth floor was covered completely in soft furs. It cushioned her feet beneath her slippers. Below the center point of the pyramid was a high platform bed, which required a step to climb onto it. Silk hung down around the sides, stirring delicately in the torchlight like soft white clouds.

She should have run *out* of the tent, not in.

Spinning to do just that, she realized the only exit was still blocked. She was trapped. Olek grinned, though the look seemed baffled.

"I-I," she stuttered, not sure how to explain her rude behavior, or if she even should.

Olek let the flap fall shut behind him as he followed her inside. He resembled a stalking beast after his prey, relishing the anticipation of the hunt.

Nadja turned from him and was again met with the giant bed. She recoiled from it as if it was covered in poison. It occurred to her how intimate this night really could be. Stumbling back, she bumped into an incredibly hard chest.

She jolted in panic, scurrying away from the solid, warm muscles. Her eyes darted around, taking in the three corners of the enclosure. In the first, there was a bath drawn, the steaming water coming out of the basin. A sweet perfumed scent rose with it. Folded towels, bath oils, and rinses were neatly arranged at the side.

The next corner had a table full of chocolates, fruits and cream sauces. A bench with cushioned seats stretched along the side, resembling a couch. An earthen wine jug was set in the center. Feeling the heady consequences of the liquor she had drunk too much of at the feast, she turned away from the food.

The third corner, behind the bed, was harder to see from her position so she ignored it. Feeling rather than hearing Olek coming up behind her, she again panicked. Swirling to face him, she held up her arms and backed away. Her hands shook. This was not how she imagined being alone with a man would feel like. She always assumed it would be like reporting to one of the robot guards, or talking to a dignitary at some function she was forced to attend.

But Olek was half naked and smiling at her like he knew every thought in her head. Did he somehow realize she liked looking at his oiled chest, to the point where she made a conscious effort not to? Could he know that when his hand had briefly held hers, her nerves had tingled, were still tingling? That the idea of his kisses both excited and terrified her?

Merriment poured from his gaze and she blushed to see it. He held back, standing tall as Nadja studied him. Before she realized it, her eyes were traveling a seductive journey of discovery over his taut chest. Already his small nipples were hard buds. His flesh dipped in all the right places only to rise and swell with each of his shallow breaths. There was no fat on his chiseled form and she doubted they employed beauty services to remove fat cells on a planet like this. His body was all natural. She bit her bottom lip, absently chewing at it as she looked him over.

His broad shoulders carried his strong arms with ease. They were arms that could crush her if he so chose. The metal band on his biceps would have fit on top of her head like a crown. Looking closer, she saw that the jewelry was shaped like a dragon winding over flesh.

Nadja looked at his covered face. He did indeed appear bold and strong like a dragon.

"Are you pleased?" he asked confidently when she didn't move. Again, his smile was alluring and light. She could tell by the expression that this was a man who laughed often.

She blinked nervously, trying to erase the image of tight flesh burning into her memory. He took a step forward, moving as if to touch her.

"No," she commanded, her eyes narrowing. Her words stopped him. Her breathing deepened. "Just stay back a moment."

His head tilted to the side, waiting for her command.

Nadja took another deep breath, trying to control her undisciplined emotions and wild heartbeat.

"I don't think there is a need to do any of..." She swallowed nervously and looked at the bath and then the bed. Shivering, she tried to lift her hands to cross protectively over her chest and grew frustrated by the binding straps. With a frown, she tugged the belt off her arms. "I meant to say, I know the tradition of this night is to prove yourself a worthy mate by a display of your..."

As Olek arched a brow, she saw the shifting beneath his mask. His eyes dipped to focus on the way her breasts bounced with her jerking movements. She freed herself from the arm ties and left them to hang at her waist.

Swallowing over her embarrassment, she crossed her arms over her chest to break his gaze, and uttered, "Your prowess."

The grin widened over his amazingly firm lips. Those lips weren't fair. No man should look that delectable. Nadja made a small sound of distress before continuing. She knew he wanted her to choose him for her husband. It wasn't fair. He couldn't really speak until she granted him permission. The only way to grant him permission was to accept him as a husband. Hurting his feelings wasn't a great way to start off their possible life together, so she tried to speak carefully.

"I am telling you, there is no need for that. I am not concerned with..." Nadja felt like kicking herself. The words sounded weak and trembling. Normally she could speak with soft confidence, always reasonable and logical and well-phrased. Her voice came out in hot, breathless pants. What was he doing to her? Her body felt like it was on fire, like she needed to take off her clothes and jump into a snow drift. She started to sweat. Absently, she fanned her face, trying to concentrate. Forgetting where she had left off, she repeated, "I am not concerned with your prowess— *ah!*"

Olek boldly whipped his loincloth from his hips and dropped it to the fur-lined floor.

To find out more about Michelle's books
visit www.MichellePillow.com

LOVE POTIONS

BY MICHELLE M. PILLOW

Warlocks MacGregor® Book 1
Contemporary Paranormal Scottish Warlocks

A little magickal mischief never hurt anyone...

Erik MacGregor, from a clan of ancient Scottish warlocks, isn't looking for love. After centuries, it's not even a consideration...until he moves in next door to Lydia Barratt. It's clear that the shy beauty wants nothing to do with him, but he's drawn to her nonetheless and determined to win her over.

Lydia Barratt just wants to be left alone to grow flowers and make lotions in her old Victorian house. The last thing she needs is a demanding Scottish man meddling in her private life. Just because he's gorgeous and totally rocks a kilt doesn't mean she's going to fall for his seductive manner.

But Erik won't give up and just as Lydia let's her guard down, his sister decides to get involved. Her little love potion prank goes terribly wrong, making Lydia the target of his sudden embarrassingly obsessive behavior. They'll have to find a way to pull Erik out of the spell fast when it becomes clear that Lydia has more than a lovesick warlock to worry about. Evil lurks within the shadows and it plans to use Lydia, alive or dead, to take out Erik and his clan for good.

Love Potions Excerpt

"Ly-di-ah! I sit beneath your window, laaaass, singing 'cause I loooove your a—""

"For the love of St. Francis of Assisi, someone call a vet. There is an injured animal screaming in pain outside," Charlotte interrupted the flow of music in ill-humor.

Lydia lifted her forehead from the kitchen table. Her windows and doors were all locked, and yet Erik's endlessly verbose singing penetrated the barrier of glass and wood with ease.

Charlotte held her head and blinked heavily. Her red-rimmed eyes were filled with the all too poignant look of a hangover. She took a seat at the table and laid her head down. Her moan sounded something like, "I'm never moving again."

"You need fluids," Lydia prescribed, getting up to pour unsweetened herbal tea from the pitcher in the fridge. She'd mixed it especially for her friend. It was Gramma Annabelle's hangover recipe of willow bark, peppermint, carrot, and ginger. The old lady always had a fresh supply of it in the house while she was alive. Apparently, being a natural witch also meant in partaking in natural liquors. Annabelle had kept a steady supply of moonshine stashed in the basement. If the concert didn't stop soon she might try to find an old bottle.

"*Ly-di-ah!*"

"Omigod. Kill me," Charlotte moaned. "No. Kill him. Then kill me."

"*Ly-di-ah!*"

Erik had been singing for over an hour. At first, he'd tried to come inside. She'd not invited him and the barrier spell sent him sprawling back into the yard. He didn't seem to mind as he found a seat on some landscaping timbers and began his serenade. The last time she'd asked him to be quiet, he'd gotten louder and overly enthusiastic. In fact, she'd been too scared to pull back the curtains for a clearer look, but she was pretty sure he'd been dancing on her lawn, shaking his kilt.

"Omigod," Charlotte muttered, pushing up and angrily going to a window. Then grimacing, she said, "Is he wearing a tux jacket with his kilt?"

"Don't let him see you," Lydia cried out in a panic. It was too late. The song began with renewed force.

"He's..." Charlotte frowned. "I think it's dancing."

Since the damage was done, Lydia joined Charlotte at the window. Erik grinned. He lifted his arms to the side and kicked his legs, bouncing around the yard like a kid on too much sugar. "Maybe it's a traditional Scottish dance?"

Both women tilted their heads in unison as his kilt kicked up to show his perfectly formed ass.

"He's not wearing..." Charlotte began.

"I know. He doesn't," Lydia answered. Damn, the man had a fine body. Too bad Malina's trick had turned him insane.

To find out more about Michelle's books visit www.MichellePillow.com

PLEASE LEAVE A REVIEW

Please take a moment to share your thoughts by
scrolling to the end of the document to rate/review
this book.
Thank you for reading!

Be sure to check out Michelle's other titles at

www.michellepillow.com